# American Indian Stories
## and
## Old Indian Legends

ZITKALA-ŠA (Gertrude Bonnin)
A Dakota Sioux Indian

*"There is no great; there is no small;
in the mind that causeth all"*

DOVER · THRIFT · EDITIONS

# American Indian Stories
# and
# Old Indian Legends

## ZITKALA-ŠA

DOVER PUBLICATIONS, INC.
Mineola, New York

# DOVER THRIFT EDITIONS

GENERAL EDITOR: MARY CAROLYN WALDREP
EDITOR OF THIS VOLUME: JANET B. KOPITO

*Bibliographical Note*

*American Indian Stories and Old Indian Legends,* first published by Dover Publications, Inc., in 2014, is a republication of the following works: *American Indian Stories,* published by Hayworth Publishing House, Washington, D.C., in 1921 and *Old Indian Legends,* published by Ginn and Company, Boston, in 1901.

*International Standard Book Number*

ISBN-13: 978-0-486-78043-6
ISBN-10: 0-486-78043-0

Manufactured in the United States by Courier Corporation
78043002   2015
www.doverpublications.com

# Introduction to the Dover Edition

ZITKALA-ŠA ("RED BIRD") was born Gertrude Simmons in 1876 on a Sioux Indian reservation in South Dakota. The year after she was born, the U.S. Congress reduced the size of the Great Sioux Reservation to 15 million acres from 134 million. Zitkala-Ša was sent as a child to a Quaker school in Indiana, where she received an education, but at the cost of being separated from her Native American traditions (a theme to which she would return again and again throughout her life). After returning to the reservation, she became aware of the conflict between the traditional Indian ways and the "white" culture she had experienced at the Quaker school. Nevertheless, Zitkala-Ša decided to go back to Indiana and continue her studies, especially in music. She received a scholarship and attended college in Indiana. A talented violinist, she performed with the New England Conservatory of Music in Boston and also taught music. At this time, she began to collect Native American tales, which she translated into English and Latin. In 1902, Zitkala-Ša married Raymond T. Bonnin, whom she had known on the Sioux reservation. The couple had a son, Raymond Ohiya Bonnin.

Zitkala-Ša was ever sensitive to the practice of forced assimilation of Native American children into the dominant white culture, and this theme surfaced in much of her autobiographical writing. The Boston publisher Ginn and Company brought out her collection of tales, *Old Indian Legends,* in 1901. Zitkala-Ša referred to the legends as "relics of our country's once virgin soil." The collection includes tales of Iktomi, the spider fairy, who encounters dancing ducks, offers his old blanket to the Great Spirit, meets a muskrat and a coyote and learns valuable lessons, as well as many other stories of magic and the getting of wisdom.

In addition to her achievement in literature, Zitkala-Ša worked on an opera, *The Sun Dance,* which was performed on the Ute Reservation in Utah. The opera was based on the Sun Dance ritual, which was banned for a time—it attracted crowds of thousands and was considered by the authorities to be both disruptive and controversial due to certain provocative aspects of the ritual. Zitkala-Ša and William Hanson, a music teacher, worked together on the opera, blending Indian music traditions with Western forms to produce the successful opera. *The Sun Dance* was performed on Broadway in 1938.

In 1921, Zitkala-Ša published *American Indian Stories* (Hayworth Publishing House), a compilation of pieces that had originally appeared in print twenty years earlier. Beginning with her earliest years on the Sioux reservation, Zitkala-Ša describes elements of her childhood and adulthood—learning Native American beliefs and rituals, going East to the missionary school, attending college—and concludes with the essay on "America's Indian Problem," in which she argues that the Native Americans in the United States have been poorly served by the Bureau of Indian Affairs, the federal agency created in 1824 to administer the Indian lands.

Zitkala-Ša was active in pursuing Native American rights and was politically outspoken at times (leading to her husband's dismissal from the Bureau of Indian Affairs). She was a member of the progressive Society of American Indians, and she and her husband founded the National Council of American Indians, with the goal of uniting the tribes in the U.S. and securing full citizenship and the right to vote. Several years before her death in 1938, Zitkala-Ša was a co-author of an article that led to the federal government's adoption of the Indian Reorganization Act, which enabled Native Americans to manage their own lands.

# Contents

# Old Indian Legends .......................... 87

# American Indian Stories
# and
# Old Indian Legends

# American Indian Stories

# IMPRESSIONS OF
# AN INDIAN CHILDHOOD

## I
## MY MOTHER

A WIGWAM OF weather-stained canvas stood at the base of some irregularly ascending hills. A footpath wound its way gently down the sloping land till it reached the broad river bottom; creeping through the long swamp grasses that bent over it on either side, it came out on the edge of the Missouri.

Here, morning, noon, and evening, my mother came to draw water from the muddy stream for our household use. Always, when my mother started for the river, I stopped my play to run along with her. She was only of medium height. Often she was sad and silent, at which times her full arched lips were compressed into hard and bitter lines, and shadows fell under her black eyes. Then I clung to her hand and begged to know what made the tears fall.

"Hush; my little daughter must never talk about my tears"; and smiling through them, she patted my head and said, "Now let me see how fast you can run today." Whereupon I tore away at my highest possible speed, with my long black hair blowing in the breeze.

I was a wild little girl of seven. Loosely clad in a slip of brown buckskin, and light-footed with a pair of soft moccasins on my feet, I was as free as the wind that blew my hair, and no less spirited than a bounding deer. These were my mother's pride,—my wild freedom and overflowing spirits. She taught me no fear save that of intruding myself upon others.

Having gone many paces ahead I stopped, panting for breath, and laughing with glee as my mother watched my every movement. I

3

was not wholly conscious of myself, but was more keenly alive to the fire within. It was as if I were the activity, and my hands and feet were only experiments for my spirit to work upon.

Returning from the river, I tugged beside my mother, with my hand upon the bucket I believed I was carrying. One time, on such a return, I remember a bit of conversation we had. My grown-up cousin, Warca-Ziwin (Sunflower), who was then seventeen, always went to the river alone for water for her mother. Their wigwam was not far from ours; and I saw her daily going to and from the river. I admired my cousin greatly. So I said: "Mother, when I am tall as my cousin Warca-Ziwin, you shall not have to come for water. I will do it for you."

With a strange tremor in her voice which I could not understand, she answered, "If the paleface does not take away from us the river we drink."

"Mother, who is this bad paleface?" I asked.

"My little daughter, he is a sham,—a sickly sham! The bronzed Dakota is the only real man."

I looked up into my mother's face while she spoke; and seeing her bite her lips, I knew she was unhappy. This aroused revenge in my small soul. Stamping my foot on the earth, I cried aloud, "I hate the paleface that makes my mother cry!"

Setting the pail of water on the ground, my mother stooped, and stretching her left hand out on the level with my eyes, she placed her other arm about me; she pointed to the hill where my uncle and my only sister lay buried.

"There is what the paleface has done! Since then your father too has been buried in a hill nearer the rising sun. We were once very happy. But the paleface has stolen our lands and driven us hither. Having defrauded us of our land, the paleface forced us away.

"Well, it happened on the day we moved camp that your sister and uncle were both very sick. Many others were ailing, but there seemed to be no help. We traveled many days and nights; not in the grand, happy way that we moved camp when I was a little girl, but we were driven, my child, driven like a herd of buffalo. With every step, your sister, who was not as large as you are now, shrieked with the painful jar until she was hoarse with crying. She grew more and more feverish. Her little hands and cheeks were burning hot. Her little lips were parched and dry, but she would not drink the water I gave her. Then I discovered that her throat was swollen and red. My poor child, how I cried with her because the Great Spirit had forgotten us!

"At last, when we reached this western country, on the first weary night your sister died. And soon your uncle died also, leaving a widow and an orphan daughter, your cousin Warca-Ziwin. Both your sister and uncle might have been happy with us today, had it not been for the heartless paleface."

My mother was silent the rest of the way to our wigwam. Though I saw no tears in her eyes, I knew that was because I was with her. She seldom wept before me.

## II.
## THE LEGENDS

During the summer days my mother built her fire in the shadow of our wigwam.

In the early morning our simple breakfast was spread upon the grass west of our tepee. At the farthest point of the shade my mother sat beside her fire, toasting a savory piece of dried meat. Near her, I sat upon my feet, eating my dried meat with unleavened bread, and drinking strong black coffee.

The morning meal was our quiet hour, when we two were entirely alone. At noon, several who chanced to be passing by stopped to rest, and to share our luncheon with us, for they were sure of our hospitality.

My uncle, whose death my mother ever lamented, was one of our nation's bravest warriors. His name was on the lips of old men when talking of the proud feats of valor; and it was mentioned by younger men, too, in connection with deeds of gallantry. Old women praised him for his kindness toward them; young women held him up as an ideal to their sweethearts. Every one loved him, and my mother worshiped his memory. Thus it happened that even strangers were sure of welcome in our lodge, if they but asked a favor in my uncle's name.

Though I heard many strange experiences related by these wayfarers, I loved best the evening meal, for that was the time old legends were told. I was always glad when the sun hung low in the west, for then my mother sent me to invite the neighboring old men and women to eat supper with us. Running all the way to the wigwams, I halted shyly at the entrances. Sometimes I stood long

moments without saying a word. It was not any fear that made me
so dumb when out upon such a happy errand; nor was it that I
wished to withhold the invitation, for it was all I could do to
observe this very proper silence. But it was a sensing of the atmosphere, to assure myself that I should not hinder other plans. My
mother used to say to me, as I was almost bounding away for the
old people: "Wait a moment before you invite any one. If other
plans are being discussed, do not interfere, but go elsewhere."

The old folks knew the meaning of my pauses; and often they
coaxed my confidence by asking, "What do you seek, little
granddaughter?"

"My mother says you are to come to our tepee this evening," I
instantly exploded, and breathed the freer afterwards.

"Yes, yes, gladly, gladly I shall come!" each replied. Rising at
once and carrying their blankets across one shoulder, they flocked
leisurely from their various wigwams toward our dwelling.

My mission done, I ran back, skipping and jumping with delight.
All out of breath, I told my mother almost the exact words of the
answers to my invitation. Frequently she asked, "What were they
doing when you entered their tepee?" This taught me to remember all I saw at a single glance. Often I told my mother my impressions without being questioned.

While in the neighboring wigwams sometimes an old Indian
woman asked me, "What is your mother doing?" Unless my
mother had cautioned me not to tell, I generally answered her
questions without reserve.

At the arrival of our guests I sat close to my mother, and did not
leave her side without first asking her consent. I ate my supper in
quiet, listening patiently to the talk of the old people, wishing all
the time that they would begin the stories I loved best. At last,
when I could not wait any longer, I whispered in my mother's ear,
"Ask them to tell an Iktomi story, mother."

Soothing my impatience, my mother said aloud, "My little
daughter is anxious to hear your legends." By this time all were
through eating, and the evening was fast deepening into twilight.

As each in turn began to tell a legend, I pillowed my head in my
mother's lap; and lying flat upon my back, I watched the stars as
they peeped down upon me, one by one. The increasing interest
of the tale aroused me, and I sat up eagerly listening for every
word. The old women made funny remarks, and laughed so heartily that I could not help joining them.

The distant howling of a pack of wolves or the hooting of an owl in the river bottom frightened me, and I nestled into my mother's lap. She added some dry sticks to the open fire, and the bright flames leaped up into the faces of the old folks as they sat around in a great circle.

On such an evening, I remember the glare of the fire shone on a tattooed star upon the brow of the old warrior who was telling a story. I watched him curiously as he made his unconscious gestures. The blue star upon his bronzed forehead was a puzzle to me. Looking about, I saw two parallel lines on the chin of one of the old women. The rest had none. I examined my mother's face, but found no sign there.

After the warrior's story was finished, I asked the old woman the meaning of the blue lines on her chin, looking all the while out of the corners of my eyes at the warrior with the star on his forehead. I was a little afraid that he would rebuke me for my boldness.

Here the old woman began: "Why, my grandchild, they are signs,—secret signs I dare not tell you. I shall, however, tell you a wonderful story about a woman who had a cross tattooed upon each of her cheeks."

It was a long story of a woman whose magic power lay hidden behind the marks upon her face. I fell asleep before the story was completed.

Ever after that night I felt suspicious of tattooed people. Whenever I saw one I glanced furtively at the mark and round about it, wondering what terrible magic power was covered there.

It was rarely that such a fearful story as this one was told by the camp fire. Its impression was so acute that the picture still remains vividly clear and pronounced.

## III.
## THE BEADWORK

Soon after breakfast, mother sometimes began her beadwork. On a bright, clear day, she pulled out the wooden pegs that pinned the skirt of our wigwam to the ground, and rolled the canvas part way up on its frame of slender poles. Then the cool morning breezes swept freely through our dwelling, now and then wafting the perfume of sweet grasses from newly burnt prairie.

Untying the long tasseled strings that bound a small brown buckskin bag, my mother spread upon a mat beside her bunches of colored beads, just as an artist arranges the paints upon his palette. On a lapboard she smoothed out a double sheet of soft white buckskin; and drawing from a beaded case that hung on the left of her wide belt a long, narrow blade, she trimmed the buckskin into shape. Often she worked upon small moccasins for her small daughter. Then I became intensely interested in her designing. With a proud, beaming face, I watched her work. In imagination, I saw myself walking in a new pair of snugly fitting moccasins. I felt the envious eyes of my playmates upon the pretty red beads decorating my feet.

Close beside my mother I sat on a rug, with a scrap of buckskin in one hand and an awl in the other. This was the beginning of my practical observation lessons in the art of beadwork. From a skein of finely twisted threads of silvery sinews my mother pulled out a single one. With an awl she pierced the buckskin, and skillfully threaded it with the white sinew. Picking up the tiny beads one by one, she strung them with the point of her thread, always twisting it carefully after every stitch.

It took many trials before I learned how to knot my sinew thread on the point of my finger, as I saw her do. Then the next difficulty was in keeping my thread stiffly twisted, so that I could easily string my beads upon it. My mother required of me original designs for my lessons in beading. At first I frequently ensnared many a sunny hour into working a long design. Soon I learned from self-inflicted punishment to refrain from drawing complex patterns, for I had to finish whatever I began.

After some experience I usually drew easy and simple crosses and squares. These were some of the set forms. My original designs were not always symmetrical nor sufficiently characteristic, two faults with which my mother had little patience. The quietness of her oversight made me feel strongly responsible and dependent upon my own judgment. She treated me as a dignified little individual as long as I was on my good behavior; and how humiliated I was when some boldness of mine drew forth a rebuke from her!

In the choice of colors she left me to my own taste. I was pleased with an outline of yellow upon a background of dark blue, or a combination of red and myrtle-green. There was another of red with a bluish gray that was more conventionally used. When I became a little familiar with designing and the various pleasing combinations of color, a harder lesson was given me. It was the sewing on, instead of beads, some tinted porcupine quills, moistened and flattened between the nails of the thumb and forefinger.

My mother cut off the prickly ends and burned them at once in the centre fire. These sharp points were poisonous, and worked into the flesh wherever they lodged. For this reason, my mother said, I should not do much alone in quills until I was as tall as my cousin Warca-Ziwin.

Always after these confining lessons I was wild with surplus spirits, and found joyous relief in running loose in the open again. Many a summer afternoon, a party of four or five of my playmates roamed over the hills with me. We each carried a light sharpened rod about four feet long, with which we pried up certain sweet roots. When we had eaten all the choice roots we chanced upon, we shouldered our rods and strayed off into patches of a stalky plant under whose yellow blossoms we found little crystal drops of gum. Drop by drop we gathered this nature's rock-candy, until each of us could boast of a lump the size of a small bird's egg. Soon satiated with its woody flavor, we tossed away our gum, to return again to the sweet roots.

I remember well how we used to exchange our necklaces, beaded belts, and sometimes even our moccasins. We pretended to offer them as gifts to one another. We delighted in impersonating our own mothers. We talked of things we had heard them say in their conversations. We imitated their various manners, even to the inflection of their voices. In the lap of the prairie we seated ourselves upon our feet; and leaning our painted cheeks in the palms of our hands, we rested our elbows on our knees, and bent forward as old women were most accustomed to do.

While one was telling of some heroic deed recently done by a near relative, the rest of us listened attentively, and exclaimed in undertones, "Han! han!" (yes! yes!) whenever the speaker paused for breath, or sometimes for our sympathy. As the discourse became more thrilling, according to our ideas, we raised our voices in these interjections. In these impersonations our parents were led to say only those things that were in common favor.

No matter how exciting a tale we might be rehearsing, the mere shifting of a cloud shadow in the landscape near by was sufficient to change our impulses; and soon we were all chasing the great shadows that played among the hills. We shouted and whooped in the chase; laughing and calling to one another, we were like little sportive nymphs on that Dakota sea of rolling green.

On one occasion I forgot the cloud shadow in a strange notion to catch up with my own shadow. Standing straight and still, I began to glide after it, putting out one foot cautiously. When, with the greatest care, I set my foot in advance of myself, my shadow crept onward too. Then again I tried it; this time with the other foot. Still again my shadow escaped me. I began to run; and away flew my shadow, always just a step beyond me. Faster and faster I ran, setting my teeth and clenching my fists, determined to overtake my own fleet shadow. But ever swifter it glided before me, while I was growing breathless and hot. Slackening my speed, I was greatly vexed that my shadow should check its pace also. Daring it to the utmost, as I thought, I sat down upon a rock imbedded in the hillside.

So! my shadow had the impudence to sit down beside me!

Now my comrades caught up with me, and began to ask why I was running away so fast.

"Oh, I was chasing my shadow! Didn't you ever do that?" I inquired, surprised that they should not understand.

They planted their moccasined feet firmly upon my shadow to stay it, and I arose. Again my shadow slipped away, and moved as often as I did. Then we gave up trying to catch my shadow.

Before this peculiar experience I have no distinct memory of having recognized any vital bond between myself and my own shadow. I never gave it an afterthought.

Returning our borrowed belts and trinkets, we rambled homeward. That evening, as on other evenings, I went to sleep over my legends.

## IV.
## THE COFFEE-MAKING

One summer afternoon, my mother left me alone in our wigwam, while she went across the way to my aunt's dwelling.

I did not much like to stay alone in our tepee, for I feared a tall, broad-shouldered crazy man, some forty years old, who walked loose among the hills. Wiyaka-Napbina (Wearer of a Feather Necklace) was harmless, and whenever he came into a wigwam he was driven there by extreme hunger. He went nude except for the half of a red blanket he girdled around his waist. In one tawny arm he used to carry a heavy bunch of wild sunflowers that he gathered in his aimless ramblings. His black hair was matted by the winds, and scorched into a dry red by the constant summer sun. As he took great strides, placing one brown bare foot directly in front of the other, he swung his long lean arm to and fro.

Frequently he paused in his walk and gazed far backward, shading his eyes with his hand. He was under the belief that an evil spirit was haunting his steps. This was what my mother told me once, when I sneered at such a silly big man. I was brave when my mother was near by, and Wiyaka-Napbina walking farther and farther away.

"Pity the man, my child. I knew him when he was a brave and handsome youth. He was overtaken by a malicious spirit among the hills, one day, when he went hither and thither after his ponies. Since then he cannot stay away from the hills," she said.

I felt so sorry for the man in his misfortune that I prayed to the Great Spirit to restore him. But though I pitied him at a distance, I was still afraid of him when he appeared near our wigwam.

Thus, when my mother left me by myself that afternoon, I sat in a fearful mood within our tepee. I recalled all I had ever heard about Wiyaka-Napbina; and I tried to assure myself that though he might pass near by, he would not come to our wigwam because there was no little girl around our grounds.

Just then, from without a hand lifted the canvas covering of the entrance; the shadow of a man fell within the wigwam, and a large roughly moccasined foot was planted inside.

For a moment I did not dare to breathe or stir, for I thought that could be no other than Wiyaka-Napbina. The next instant I sighed aloud in relief. It was an old grandfather who had often told me Iktomi legends.

"Where is your mother, my little grandchild?" were his first words.

"My mother is soon coming back from my aunt's tepee," I replied.

"Then I shall wait awhile for her return," he said, crossing his feet and seating himself upon a mat.

At once I began to play the part of a generous hostess. I turned to my mother's coffeepot.

Lifting the lid, I found nothing but coffee grounds in the bottom. I set the pot on a heap of cold ashes in the centre, and filled it half full of warm Missouri River water. During this performance I felt conscious of being watched. Then breaking off a small piece of our unleavened bread, I placed it in a bowl. Turning soon to the coffeepot, which would never have boiled on a dead fire had I waited forever, I poured out a cup of worse than muddy warm water. Carrying the bowl in one hand and cup in the other, I handed the light luncheon to the old warrior. I offered them to him with the air of bestowing generous hospitality.

"How! how!" he said, and placed the dishes on the ground in front of his crossed feet. He nibbled at the bread and sipped from the cup. I sat back against a pole watching him. I was proud to have succeeded so well in serving refreshments to a guest all by myself. Before the old warrior had finished eating, my mother entered. Immediately she wondered where I had found coffee, for she knew I had never made any, and that she had left the coffeepot empty. Answering the question in my mother's eyes, the warrior remarked, "My granddaughter made coffee on a heap of dead ashes, and served me the moment I came."

They both laughed, and mother said, "Wait a little longer, and I shall build a fire." She meant to make some real coffee. But neither she nor the warrior, whom the law of our custom had compelled to partake of my insipid hospitality, said anything to embarrass me. They treated my best judgment, poor as it was, with the utmost respect. It was not till long years afterward that I learned how ridiculous a thing I had done.

## V.
## THE DEAD MAN'S PLUM BUSH

One autumn afternoon, many people came streaming toward the dwelling of our near neighbor. With painted faces, and wearing broad white bosoms of elk's teeth, they hurried down the narrow footpath to Haraka Wambdi's wigwam. Young mothers had their children by the hand, and half pulled them along in their haste. They overtook and passed by the bent old grandmothers who were trudging along with crooked canes toward the centre of excitement. Most of the young braves galloped hither on their ponies. Toothless warriors, like the old women, came more slowly, though mounted on lively ponies. They sat proudly erect on their horses. They wore their eagle plumes, and waved their various trophies of former wars.

In front of the wigwam a great fire was built, and several large black kettles of venison were suspended over it. The crowd were seated about it on the grass in a great circle. Behind them some of the braves stood leaning against the necks of their ponies, their tall figures draped in loose robes which were well drawn over their eyes.

Young girls, with their faces glowing like bright red autumn leaves, their glossy braids falling over each ear, sat coquettishly beside their chaperons. It was a custom for young Indian women to invite some older relative to escort them to the public feasts. Though it was not an iron law, it was generally observed.

Haraka Wambdi was a strong young brave, who had just returned from his first battle, a warrior. His near relatives, to celebrate his new rank, were spreading a feast to which the whole of the Indian village was invited.

Holding my pretty striped blanket in readiness to throw over my shoulders, I grew more and more restless as I watched the gay throng assembling. My mother was busily broiling a wild duck that my aunt had that morning brought over.

"Mother, mother, why do you stop to cook a small meal when we are invited to a feast?" I asked, with a snarl in my voice.

"My child, learn to wait. On our way to the celebration we are going to stop at Chanyu's wigwam. His aged mother-in-law is lying very ill, and I think she would like a taste of this small game."

Having once seen the suffering on the thin, pinched features of this dying woman, I felt a momentary shame that I had not remembered her before.

On our way I ran ahead of my mother, and was reaching out my hand to pick some purple plums that grew on a small bush, when I was checked by a low "Sh!" from my mother.

"Why, mother, I want to taste the plums!" I exclaimed, as I dropped my hand to my side in disappointment.

"Never pluck a single plum from this bush, my child, for its roots are wrapped around an Indian's skeleton. A brave is buried here. While he lived, he was so fond of playing the game of striped plum seeds that, at his death, his set of plum seeds were buried in his hands. From them sprang up this little bush."

Eyeing the forbidden fruit, I trod lightly on the sacred ground, and dared to speak only in whispers, until we had gone many paces from it. After that time, I halted in my ramblings whenever I came in sight of the plum bush. I grew sober with awe, and was alert to hear a long-drawn-out whistle rise from the roots of it. Though I had never heard with my own ears this strange whistle of departed spirits, yet I had listened so frequently to hear the old folks describe it that I knew I should recognize it at once.

The lasting impression of that day, as I recall it now, is what my mother told me about the dead man's plum bush.

# VI.
## THE GROUND SQUIRREL

In the busy autumn days, my cousin Warca-Ziwin's mother came to our wigwam to help my mother preserve foods for our winter use. I was very fond of my aunt, because she was not so quiet as my mother. Though she was older, she was more jovial and less reserved. She was slender and remarkably erect. While my mother's hair was heavy and black, my aunt had unusually thin locks.

Ever since I knew her she wore a string of large blue beads around her neck,—beads that were precious because my uncle had given them to her when she was a younger woman. She had a peculiar swing in her gait, caused by a long stride rarely natural to so slight a figure. It was during my aunt's visit with us that my mother forgot her accustomed quietness, often laughing heartily at some of my aunt's witty remarks.

I loved my aunt threefold: for her hearty laughter, for the cheerfulness she caused my mother, and most of all for the times she dried my tears and held me in her lap, when my mother had reproved me.

Early in the cool mornings, just as the yellow rim of the sun rose above the hills, we were up and eating our breakfast. We awoke so early that we saw the sacred hour when a misty smoke hung over a pit surrounded by an impassable sinking mire. This strange smoke appeared every morning, both winter and summer; but most visibly in midwinter it rose immediately above the marshy spot. By the time the full face of the sun appeared above the eastern horizon, the smoke vanished. Even very old men, who had known this country the longest, said that the smoke from this pit had never failed a single day to rise heavenward.

As I frolicked about our dwelling I used to stop suddenly, and with a fearful awe watch the smoking of the unknown fires. While the vapor was visible I was afraid to go very far from our wigwam unless I went with my mother.

From a field in the fertile river bottom my mother and aunt gathered an abundant supply of corn. Near our tepee, they spread a large canvas upon the grass, and dried their sweet corn in it. I was left to watch the corn, that nothing should disturb it. I played around it with dolls made of ears of corn. I braided their soft fine silk for hair, and gave them blankets as various as the scraps I found in my mother's workbag.

There was a little stranger with a black-and-yellow-striped coat that used to come to the drying corn. It was a little ground squirrel, who was so fearless of me that he came to one corner of the canvas and carried away as much of the sweet corn as he could hold. I wanted very much to catch him and rub his pretty fur back, but my mother said he would be so frightened if I caught him that he would bite my fingers. So I was as content as he to keep the corn between us. Every morning he came for more corn. Some evenings I have seen him creeping about our grounds; and when I gave a sudden whoop of recognition he ran quickly out of sight.

When mother had dried all the corn she wished, then she sliced great pumpkins into thin rings; and these she doubled and linked together into long chains. She hung them on a pole that stretched between two forked posts. The wind and sun soon thoroughly dried the chains of pumpkin. Then she packed them away in a case of thick and stiff buckskin.

In the sun and wind she also dried many wild fruits,—cherries, berries, and plums. But chiefest among my early recollections of autumn is that one of the corn drying and the ground squirrel.

I have few memories of winter days at this period of my life, though many of the summer. There is one only which I can recall.

Some missionaries gave me a little bag of marbles. They were all sizes and colors. Among them were some of colored glass. Walking with my mother to the river, on a late winter day, we found great chunks of ice piled all along the bank. The ice on the river was floating in huge pieces. As I stood beside one large block, I noticed for the first time the colors of the rainbow in the crystal ice. Immediately I thought of my glass marbles at home. With my bare fingers I tried to pick out some of the colors, for they seemed so near the surface. But my fingers began to sting with the intense cold, and I had to bite them hard to keep from crying.

From that day on, for many a moon, I believed that glass marbles had river ice inside of them.

# VII.
## THE BIG RED APPLES

The first turning away from the easy, natural flow of my life occurred in an early spring. It was in my eighth year; in the month of March, I afterward learned. At this age I knew but one language, and that was my mother's native tongue.

From some of my playmates I heard that two paleface missionaries were in our village. They were from that class of white men who wore big hats and carried large hearts, they said. Running direct to my mother, I began to question her why these two strangers were among us. She told me, after I had teased much, that they had come to take away Indian boys and girls to the East. My mother did not seem to want me to talk about them. But in a day or two, I gleaned many wonderful stories from my playfellows concerning the strangers.

"Mother, my friend Judéwin is going home with the missionaries. She is going to a more beautiful country than ours; the palefaces told her so!" I said wistfully, wishing in my heart that I too might go.

Mother sat in a chair, and I was hanging on her knee. Within the last two seasons my big brother Dawée had returned from a three years' education in the East, and his coming back influenced my mother to take a farther step from her native way of living. First it was a change from the buffalo skin to the white man's canvas that covered our wigwam. Now she had given up her wigwam of slender poles, to live, a foreigner, in a home of clumsy logs.

"Yes, my child, several others besides Judéwin are going away with the palefaces. Your brother said the missionaries had inquired about his little sister," she said, watching my face very closely.

My heart thumped so hard against my breast, I wondered if she could hear it.

"Did he tell them to take me, mother?" I asked, fearing lest Dawée had forbidden the palefaces to see me, and that my hope of going to the Wonderland would be entirely blighted.

With a sad, slow smile, she answered: "There! I knew you were wishing to go, because Judéwin has filled your ears with the white man's lies. Don't believe a word they say! Their words are sweet, but, my child, their deeds are bitter. You will cry for me, but they will not even soothe you. Stay with me, my little one! Your brother Dawée says that going East, away from your mother, is too hard an experience for his baby sister."

Thus my mother discouraged my curiosity about the lands beyond our eastern horizon; for it was not yet an ambition for Letters that was stirring me. But on the following day the missionaries did come to our very house. I spied them coming up the footpath leading to our cottage. A third man was with them, but he was not my brother Dawée. It was another, a young interpreter, a paleface who had a smattering of the Indian language. I was ready to run out to meet them, but I did not dare to displease my mother. With great glee, I jumped up and down on our ground floor. I begged my mother to open the door, that they would be sure to come to us. Alas! They came, they saw, and they conquered!

Judéwin had told me of the great tree where grew red, red apples; and how we could reach out our hands and pick all the red apples we could eat. I had never seen apple trees. I had never tasted more than a dozen red apples in my life; and when I heard of the orchards of the East, I was eager to roam among them. The missionaries smiled into my eyes, and patted my head. I wondered how mother could say such hard words against him.

"Mother, ask them if little girls may have all the red apples they want, when they go East," I whispered aloud, in my excitement.

The interpreter heard me, and answered: "Yes, little girl, the nice red apples are for those who pick them; and you will have a ride on the iron horse if you go with these good people."

I had never seen a train, and he knew it.

"Mother, I am going East! I like big red apples, and I want to ride on the iron horse! Mother, say yes!" I pleaded.

My mother said nothing. The missionaries waited in silence; and my eyes began to blur with tears, though I struggled to choke them back. The corners of my mouth twitched, and my mother saw me.

"I am not ready to give you any word," she said to them. "Tomorrow I shall send you my answer by my son."

With this they left us. Alone with my mother, I yielded to my tears, and cried aloud, shaking my head so as not to hear what she was saying to me. This was the first time I had ever been so unwilling to give up my own desire that I refused to hearken to my mother's voice.

There was a solemn silence in our home that night. Before I went to bed I begged the Great Spirit to make my mother willing I should go with the missionaries.

The next morning came, and my mother called me to her side. "My daughter, do you still persist in wishing to leave your mother?" she asked.

"Oh, mother, it is not that I wish to leave you, but I want to see the wonderful Eastern land," I answered.

My dear old aunt came to our house that morning, and I heard her say, "Let her try it."

I hoped that, as usual, my aunt was pleading on my side. My brother Dawée came for mother's decision. I dropped my play, and crept close to my aunt.

"Yes, Dawée, my daughter, though she does not understand what it all means, is anxious to go. She will need an education when she is grown, for then there will be fewer real Dakotas, and many more palefaces. This tearing her away, so young, from her mother is necessary, if I would have her an educated woman. The palefaces, who owe us a large debt for stolen lands, have begun to pay a tardy justice in offering some education to our children. But I know my daughter must suffer keenly in this experiment. For her sake, I dread to tell you my reply to the missionaries. Go, tell them that they may take my little daughter, and that the Great Spirit shall not fail to reward them according to their hearts."

Wrapped in my heavy blanket, I walked with my mother to the carriage that was soon to take us to the iron horse. I was happy. I met my playmates, who were also wearing their best thick blankets. We showed one another our new beaded moccasins, and the width of the belts that girdled our new dresses. Soon we were being drawn rapidly away by the white man's horses. When I saw the lonely figure of my mother vanish in the distance, a sense of regret settled heavily upon me. I felt suddenly weak, as if I might fall limp to the ground. I was in the hands of strangers whom my mother did not fully trust. I no longer felt free to be myself, or to voice my own feelings. The tears trickled down my cheeks, and I buried my face in the folds of my blanket. Now the first step, parting me from my mother, was taken, and all my belated tears availed nothing.

Having driven thirty miles to the ferryboat, we crossed the Missouri in the evening. Then riding again a few miles eastward, we stopped before a massive brick building. I looked at it in amazement and with a vague misgiving, for in our village I had never seen so large a house. Trembling with fear and distrust of the palefaces, my teeth chattering from the chilly ride, I crept noiselessly in my soft moccasins along the narrow hall, keeping very close to the bare wall. I was as frightened and bewildered as the captured young of a wild creature.

# THE SCHOOL DAYS OF AN
# INDIAN GIRL

## I.
### THE LAND OF RED APPLES

THERE WERE EIGHT in our party of bronzed children who were going East with the missionaries. Among us were three young braves, two tall girls, and we three little ones, Judéwin, Thowin, and I.

We had been very impatient to start on our journey to the Red Apple Country, which, we were told, lay a little beyond the great circular horizon of the Western prairie. Under a sky of rosy apples we dreamt of roaming as freely and happily as we had chased the cloud shadows on the Dakota plains. We had anticipated much pleasure from a ride on the iron horse, but the throngs of staring palefaces disturbed and troubled us.

On the train, fair women, with tottering babies on each arm, stopped their haste and scrutinized the children of absent mothers. Large men, with heavy bundles in their hands, halted near by, and riveted their glassy blue eyes upon us.

I sank deep into the corner of my seat, for I resented being watched. Directly in front of me, children who were no larger than I hung themselves upon the backs of their seats, with their bold white faces toward me. Sometimes they took their forefingers out of their mouths and pointed at my moccasined feet. Their mothers, instead of reproving such rude curiosity, looked closely at me, and attracted their children's further notice to my blanket. This embarrassed me, and kept me constantly on the verge of tears.

I sat perfectly still, with my eyes downcast, daring only now and then to shoot long glances around me. Chancing to turn to the window at my side, I was quite breathless upon seeing one familiar object. It was the telegraph pole which strode by at short paces. Very near my mother's dwelling, along the edge of a road thickly bordered with wild sunflowers, some poles like these had been planted by white men. Often I had stopped, on my way down the road, to hold my ear against the pole, and, hearing its low moaning, I used to wonder what the paleface had done to hurt it. Now I sat watching for each pole that glided by to be the last one.

In this way I had forgotten my uncomfortable surroundings, when I heard one of my comrades call out my name. I saw the missionary standing very near, tossing candies and gums into our midst. This amused us all, and we tried to see who could catch the most of the sweetmeats.

Though we rode several days inside of the iron horse, I do not recall a single thing about our luncheons.

It was night when we reached the school grounds. The lights from the windows of the large buildings fell upon some of the icicled trees that stood beneath them. We were led toward an open door, where the brightness of the lights within flooded out over the heads of the excited palefaces who blocked our way. My body trembled more from fear than from the snow I trod upon.

Entering the house, I stood close against the wall. The strong glaring light in the large whitewashed room dazzled my eyes. The noisy hurrying of hard shoes upon a bare wooden floor increased the whirring in my ears. My only safety seemed to be in keeping next to the wall. As I was wondering in which direction to escape from all this confusion, two warm hands grasped me firmly, and in the same moment I was tossed high in midair. A rosy-cheeked paleface woman caught me in her arms. I was both frightened and insulted by such trifling. I stared into her eyes, wishing her to let me stand on my own feet, but she jumped me up and down with increasing enthusiasm. My mother had never made a plaything of her wee daughter. Remembering this I began to cry aloud.

They misunderstood the cause of my tears, and placed me at a white table loaded with food. There our party were united again. As I did not hush my crying, one of the older ones whispered to me, "Wait until you are alone in the night."

It was very little I could swallow besides my sobs, that evening.

"Oh, I want my mother and my brother Dawée! I want to go to my aunt!" I pleaded; but the ears of the palefaces could not hear me.

From the table we were taken along an upward incline of wooden boxes, which I learned afterward to call a stairway. At the top was a quiet hall, dimly lighted. Many narrow beds were in one straight line down the entire length of the wall. In them lay sleeping brown faces, which peeped just out of the coverings. I was tucked into bed with one of the tall girls, because she talked to me in my mother tongue and seemed to soothe me.

I had arrived in the wonderful land of rosy skies, but I was not happy, as I had thought I should be. My long travel and the bewildering sights had exhausted me. I fell asleep, heaving deep, tired sobs. My tears were left to dry themselves in streaks, because neither my aunt nor my mother was near to wipe them away.

## II.
## THE CUTTING OF MY LONG HAIR

The first day in the land of apples was a bitter-cold one; for the snow still covered the ground, and the trees were bare. A large bell rang for breakfast, its loud metallic voice crashing through the belfry overhead and into our sensitive ears. The annoying clatter of shoes on bare floors gave us no peace. The constant clash of harsh noises, with an undercurrent of many voices murmuring an unknown tongue, made a bedlam within which I was securely tied. And though my spirit tore itself in struggling for its lost freedom, all was useless.

A paleface woman, with white hair, came up after us. We were placed in a line of girls who were marching into the dining room. These were Indian girls, in stiff shoes and closely clinging dresses. The small girls wore sleeved aprons and shingled hair. As I walked noiselessly in my soft moccasins, I felt like sinking to the floor, for my blanket had been stripped from my shoulders. I looked hard at the Indian girls, who seemed not to care that they were even more immodestly dressed than I, in their tightly fitting clothes. While we marched in, the boys entered at an opposite door. I watched for the three young braves who came in our party. I spied them in the rear ranks, looking as uncomfortable as I felt.

A small bell was tapped, and each of the pupils drew a chair from under the table. Supposing this act meant they were to be seated, I pulled out mine and at once slipped into it from one side. But when I turned my head, I saw that I was the only one seated, and all the rest at our table remained standing. Just as I began to rise, looking shyly around to see how chairs were to be used, a second bell was sounded. All were seated at last, and I had to crawl back into my chair again. I heard a man's voice at one end of the hall, and I looked around to see him. But all the others hung their heads over their plates. As I glanced at the long chain of tables, I caught the eyes of a paleface woman upon me. Immediately I dropped my eyes, wondering why I was so keenly watched by the strange woman. The man ceased his mutterings, and then a third bell was tapped. Every one picked up his knife and fork and began eating. I began crying instead, for by this time I was afraid to venture anything more.

But this eating by formula was not the hardest trial in that first day. Late in the morning, my friend Judéwin gave me a terrible warning. Judéwin knew a few words of English, and she had overheard the paleface woman talk about cutting our long, heavy hair. Our mothers had taught us that only unskilled warriors who were captured had their hair shingled by the enemy. Among our people, short hair was worn by mourners, and shingled hair by cowards!

We discussed our fate some moments, and when Judéwin said, "We have to submit, because they are strong," I rebelled.

"No, I will not submit! I will struggle first!" I answered.

I watched my chance, and when no one noticed I disappeared. I crept up the stairs as quietly as I could in my squeaking shoes,— my moccasins had been exchanged for shoes. Along the hall I passed, without knowing whither I was going. Turning aside to an open door, I found a large room with three white beds in it. The windows were covered with dark green curtains, which made the room very dim. Thankful that no one was there, I directed my steps toward the corner farthest from the door. On my hands and knees I crawled under the bed, and cuddled myself in the dark corner.

From my hiding place I peered out, shuddering with fear whenever I heard footsteps near by. Though in the hall loud voices were calling my name, and I knew that even Judéwin was searching for me, I did not open my mouth to answer. Then the steps were quickened and the voices became excited. The sounds came nearer and nearer. Women and girls entered the room. I held my breath, and watched them open closet doors and peep behind large trunks. Some one threw up the curtains, and the room was filled with sudden light. What caused them to stoop and look under the bed I do not know. I remember being dragged out, though I resisted by kicking and scratching wildly. In spite of myself, I was carried downstairs and tied fast in a chair.

I cried aloud, shaking my head all the while until I felt the cold blades of the scissors against my neck, and heard them gnaw off one of my thick braids. Then I lost my spirit. Since the day I was taken from my mother I had suffered extreme indignities. People had stared at me. I had been tossed about in the air like a wooden puppet. And now my long hair was shingled like a coward's! In my anguish I moaned for my mother, but no one came to comfort me. Not a soul reasoned quietly with me, as my own mother used to do; for now I was only one of many little animals driven by a herder.

## III.
## THE SNOW EPISODE

A short time after our arrival we three Dakotas were playing in the snowdrift. We were all still deaf to the English language, excepting Judéwin, who always heard such puzzling things. One morning we learned through her ears that we were forbidden to fall lengthwise in the snow, as we had been doing, to see our own impressions. However, before many hours we had forgotten the order, and were having great sport in the snow, when a shrill voice called us. Looking up, we saw an imperative hand beckoning us into the house. We shook the snow off ourselves, and started toward the woman as slowly as we dared.

Judéwin said: "Now the paleface is angry with us. She is going to punish us for falling into the snow. If she looks straight into your eyes and talks loudly, you must wait until she stops. Then, after a tiny pause, say, 'No.'" The rest of the way we practiced upon the little word "no."

As it happened, Thowin was summoned to judgment first. The door shut behind her with a click.

Judéwin and I stood silently listening at the keyhole. The paleface woman talked in very severe tones. Her words fell from her lips like crackling embers, and her inflection ran up like the small end of a switch. I understood her voice better than the things she was saying. I was certain we had made her very impatient with us. Judéwin heard enough of the words to realize all too late that she had taught us the wrong reply.

"Oh, poor Thowin!" she gasped, as she put both hands over her ears.

Just then I heard Thowin's tremulous answer, "No."

With an angry exclamation, the woman gave her a hard spanking. Then she stopped to say something. Judéwin said it was this: "Are you going to obey my word the next time?"

Thowin answered again with the only word at her command, "No."

This time the woman meant her blows to smart, for the poor frightened girl shrieked at the top of her voice. In the midst of the whipping the blows ceased abruptly, and the woman asked another question: "Are you going to fall in the snow again?"

Thowin gave her bad password another trial. We heard her say feebly, "No! No!"

With this the woman hid away her half-worn slipper, and led the child out, stroking her black shorn head. Perhaps it occurred to her that brute force is not the solution for such a problem. She did nothing to Judéwin nor to me. She only returned to us our unhappy comrade, and left us alone in the room.

During the first two or three seasons misunderstandings as ridiculous as this one of the snow episode frequently took place, bringing unjustifiable frights and punishments into our little lives.

Within a year I was able to express myself somewhat in broken English. As soon as I comprehended a part of what was said and done, a mischievous spirit of revenge possessed me. One day I was called in from my play for some misconduct. I had disregarded a rule which seemed to me very needlessly binding. I was sent into the kitchen to mash the turnips for dinner. It was noon, and steaming dishes were hastily carried into the dining-room. I hated turnips, and their odor which came from the brown jar was offensive to me. With fire in my heart, I took the wooden tool that the paleface woman held out to me. I stood upon a step, and, grasping the handle with both hands, I bent in hot rage over the turnips. I worked my vengeance upon them. All were so busily occupied that no one noticed me. I saw that the turnips were in a pulp, and that further beating could not improve them; but the order was, "Mash these turnips," and mash them I would! I renewed my energy; and as I sent the masher into the bottom of the jar, I felt a satisfying sensation that the weight of my body had gone into it.

Just here a paleface woman came up to my table. As she looked into the jar she shoved my hands roughly aside. I stood fearless and angry. She placed her red hands upon the rim of the jar. Then she gave one lift and strode away from the table. But lo! the pulpy contents fell through the crumbled bottom to the floor! She spared me no scolding phrases that I had earned. I did not heed them. I felt triumphant in my revenge, though deep within me I was a wee bit sorry to have broken the jar.

As I sat eating my dinner, and saw that no turnips were served, I whooped in my heart for having once asserted the rebellion within me.

## IV.
## THE DEVIL

Among the legends the old warriors used to tell me were many stories of evil spirits. But I was taught to fear them no more than those who stalked about in material guise. I never knew there was an insolent chieftain among the bad spirits, who dared to array his forces against the Great Spirit, until I heard this white man's legend from a paleface woman.

Out of a large book she showed me a picture of the white man's devil. I looked in horror upon the strong claws that grew out of his fur-covered fingers. His feet were like his hands. Trailing at his heels was a scaly tail tipped with a serpent's open jaws. His face was a patchwork: he had bearded cheeks, like some I had seen palefaces wear; his nose was an eagle's bill, and his sharp-pointed ears were pricked up like those of a sly fox. Above them a pair of cow's horns curved upward. I trembled with awe, and my heart throbbed in my throat, as I looked at the king of evil spirits. Then I heard the paleface woman say that this terrible creature roamed loose in the world, and that little girls who disobeyed school regulations were to be tortured by him.

That night I dreamt about this evil divinity. Once again I seemed to be in my mother's cottage. An Indian woman had come to visit my mother. On opposite sides of the kitchen stove, which stood in the centre of the small house, my mother and her guest were seated in straight-backed chairs. I played with a train of empty spools hitched together on a string. It was night, and the wick burned feebly. Suddenly I heard some one turn our door-knob from without.

My mother and the woman hushed their talk, and both looked toward the door. It opened gradually. I waited behind the stove. The hinges squeaked as the door was slowly, very slowly pushed inward.

Then in rushed the devil! He was tall! He looked exactly like the picture I had seen of him in the white man's papers. He did not speak to my mother, because he did not know the Indian language, but his glittering yellow eyes were fastened upon me. He took long strides around the stove, passing behind the woman's chair. I threw down my spools, and ran to my mother. He did not fear her, but followed closely after me. Then I ran round and round the stove, crying aloud for help. But my mother and the woman seemed not to know my danger. They sat still, looking quietly upon the devil's chase after me. At last I grew dizzy. My head revolved as on a hidden pivot. My knees became numb, and doubled under my weight like a pair of knife blades without a spring. Beside my mother's chair I fell in a heap. Just as the devil stooped over me with outstretched claws my mother awoke from her quiet indifference, and lifted me on her lap. Whereupon the devil vanished, and I was awake.

On the following morning I took my revenge upon the devil. Stealing into the room where a wall of shelves was filled with books, I drew forth The Stories of the Bible. With a broken slate pencil I carried in my apron pocket, I began by scratching out his wicked eyes. A few moments later, when I was ready to leave the room, there was a ragged hole in the page where the picture of the devil had once been.

## V.
## IRON ROUTINE

A loud-clamoring bell awakened us at half-past six in the cold winter mornings. From happy dreams of Western rolling lands and unlassoed freedom we tumbled out upon chilly bare floors back again into a paleface day. We had short time to jump into our shoes and clothes, and wet our eyes with icy water, before a small hand bell was vigorously rung for roll call.

There were too many drowsy children and too numerous orders for the day to waste a moment in any apology to nature for giving her children such a shock in the early morning. We rushed downstairs, bounding over two high steps at a time, to land in the assembly room.

A paleface woman, with a yellow-covered roll book open on her arm and a gnawed pencil in her hand, appeared at the door. Her small, tired face was coldly lighted with a pair of large gray eyes.

She stood still in a halo of authority, while over the rim of her spectacles her eyes pried nervously about the room. Having glanced at her long list of names and called out the first one, she tossed up her chin and peered through the crystals of her spectacles to make sure of the answer "Here."

Relentlessly her pencil black-marked our daily records if we were not present to respond to our names, and no chum of ours had done it successfully for us. No matter if a dull headache or the painful cough of slow consumption had delayed the absentee, there was only time enough to mark the tardiness. It was next to impossible to leave the iron routine after the civilizing machine had once begun its day's buzzing; and as it was inbred in me to suffer in silence rather than to appeal to the ears of one whose open eyes could not see my pain, I have many times trudged in the day's harness heavy-footed, like a dumb sick brute.

Once I lost a dear classmate. I remember well how she used to mope along at my side, until one morning she could not raise her head from her pillow. At her deathbed I stood weeping, as the paleface woman sat near her moistening the dry lips. Among the folds of the bedclothes I saw the open pages of the white man's Bible. The dying Indian girl talked disconnectedly of Jesus the Christ and the paleface who was cooling her swollen hands and feet.

I grew bitter, and censured the woman for cruel neglect of our physical ills. I despised the pencils that moved automatically, and the one teaspoon which dealt out, from a large bottle, healing to a row of variously ailing Indian children. I blamed the hard-working, well-meaning, ignorant woman who was inculcating in our hearts her superstitious ideas. Though I was sullen in all my little troubles, as soon as I felt better I was ready again to smile upon the cruel woman. Within a week I was again actively testing the chains which tightly bound my individuality like a mummy for burial.

The melancholy of those black days has left so long a shadow that it darkens the path of years that have since gone by. These sad memories rise above those of smoothly grinding school days. Perhaps my Indian nature is the moaning wind which stirs them now for their present record. But, however tempestuous this is within me, it comes out as the low voice of a curiously colored seashell, which is only for those ears that are bent with compassion to hear it.

## VI.
## FOUR STRANGE SUMMERS

After my first three years of school, I roamed again in the Western country through four strange summers.

During this time I seemed to hang in the heart of chaos, beyond the touch or voice of human aid. My brother, being almost ten years my senior, did not quite understand my feelings. My mother had never gone inside of a schoolhouse, and so she was not capable of comforting her daughter who could read and write. Even nature seemed to have no place for me. I was neither a wee girl nor a tall one; neither a wild Indian nor a tame one. This deplorable situation was the effect of my brief course in the East, and the unsatisfactory "teenth" in a girl's years.

It was under these trying conditions that, one bright afternoon, as I sat restless and unhappy in my mother's cabin, I caught the sound of the spirited step of my brother's pony on the road which passed by our dwelling. Soon I heard the wheels of a light buckboard, and Dawée's familiar "Ho!" to his pony. He alighted upon the bare ground in front of our house. Tying his pony to one of the projecting corner logs of the low-roofed cottage, he stepped upon the wooden doorstep.

I met him there with a hurried greeting, and as I passed by, he looked a quiet "What?" into my eyes.

When he began talking with my mother, I slipped the rope from the pony's bridle. Seizing the reins and bracing my feet against the dashboard, I wheeled around in an instant. The pony was ever ready to try his speed. Looking backward, I saw Dawée waving his hand to me. I turned with the curve in the road and disappeared. I followed the winding road which crawled upward between the bases of little hillocks. Deep water-worn ditches ran parallel on either side. A strong wind blew against my cheeks and fluttered my sleeves. The pony reached the top of the highest hill, and began an even race on the level lands. There was nothing moving within that great circular horizon of the Dakota prairies save the tall grasses, over which the wind blew and rolled off in long, shadowy waves.

Within this vast wigwam of blue and green I rode reckless and insignificant. It satisfied my small consciousness to see the white foam fly from the pony's mouth.

Suddenly, out of the earth a coyote came forth at a swinging trot that was taking the cunning thief toward the hills and the village beyond. Upon the moment's impulse, I gave him a long chase and a wholesome fright. As I turned away to go back to the village, the wolf sank down upon his haunches for rest, for it was a hot summer day; and as I drove slowly homeward, I saw his sharp nose still pointed at me, until I vanished below the margin of the hilltops.

In a little while I came in sight of my mother's house. Dawée stood in the yard, laughing at an old warrior who was pointing his forefinger, and again waving his whole hand, toward the hills. With his blanket drawn over one shoulder, he talked and motioned excitedly. Dawée turned the old man by the shoulder and pointed me out to him.

"Oh han!" (Oh yes) the warrior muttered, and went his way. He had climbed the top of his favorite barren hill to survey the surrounding prairies, when he spied my chase after the coyote. His keen eyes recognized the pony and driver. At once uneasy for my safety, he had come running to my mother's cabin to give her warning. I did not appreciate his kindly interest, for there was an unrest gnawing at my heart.

As soon as he went away, I asked Dawée about something else.

"No, my baby sister, I cannot take you with me to the party tonight," he replied. Though I was not far from fifteen, and I felt that before long I should enjoy all the privileges of my tall cousin, Dawée persisted in calling me his baby sister.

That moonlight night, I cried in my mother's presence when I heard the jolly young people pass by our cottage. They were no more young braves in blankets and eagle plumes, nor Indian maids with prettily painted cheeks. They had gone three years to school in the East, and had become civilized. The young men wore the white man's coat and trousers, with bright neckties. The girls wore tight muslin dresses, with ribbons at neck and waist. At these gatherings they talked English. I could speak English almost as well as my brother, but I was not properly dressed to be taken along. I had no hat, no ribbons, and no close-fitting gown. Since my return from school I had thrown away my shoes, and wore again the soft moccasins.

While Dawée was busily preparing to go I controlled my tears. But when I heard him bounding away on his pony, I buried my face in my arms and cried hot tears.

My mother was troubled by my unhappiness. Coming to my side, she offered me the only printed matter we had in our home. It was an Indian Bible, given her some years ago by a missionary. She tried to console me. "Here, my child, are the white man's papers. Read a little from them," she said most piously.

I took it from her hand, for her sake; but my enraged spirit felt more like burning the book, which afforded me no help, and was a perfect delusion to my mother. I did not read it, but laid it unopened on the floor, where I sat on my feet. The dim yellow light of the braided muslin burning in a small vessel of oil flickered and sizzled in the awful silent storm which followed my rejection of the Bible.

Now my wrath against the fates consumed my tears before they reached my eyes. I sat stony, with a bowed head. My mother threw a shawl over her head and shoulders, and stepped out into the night.

After an uncertain solitude, I was suddenly aroused by a loud cry piercing the night. It was my mother's voice wailing among the barren hills which held the bones of buried warriors. She called aloud for her brothers' spirits to support her in her helpless misery. My fingers grew icy cold, as I realized that my unrestrained tears had betrayed my suffering to her, and she was grieving for me.

Before she returned, though I knew she was on her way, for she had ceased her weeping, I extinguished the light, and leaned my head on the window sill.

Many schemes of running away from my surroundings hovered about in my mind. A few more moons of such a turmoil drove me away to the eastern school. I rode on the white man's iron steed, thinking it would bring me back to my mother in a few winters, when I should be grown tall, and there would be congenial friends awaiting me.

## VII.
## INCURRING MY MOTHER'S DISPLEASURE

In the second journey to the East I had not come without some precautions. I had a secret interview with one of our best medicine men, and when I left his wigwam I carried securely in my sleeve a tiny bunch of magic roots. This possession assured me of friends wherever I should go. So absolutely did I believe in its charms that I wore it through all the school routine for more than a year. Then, before I lost my faith in the dead roots, I lost the little buckskin bag containing all my good luck.

At the close of this second term of three years I was the proud owner of my first diploma. The following autumn I ventured upon a college career against my mother's will.

I had written for her approval, but in her reply I found no encouragement. She called my notice to her neighbors' children, who had completed their education in three years. They had returned to their homes, and were then talking English with the frontier settlers. Her few words hinted that I had better give up my slow attempt to learn the white man's ways, and be content to roam over the prairies and find my living upon wild roots. I silenced her by deliberate disobedience.

Thus, homeless and heavy-hearted, I began anew my life among strangers.

As I hid myself in my little room in the college dormitory, away from the scornful and yet curious eyes of the students, I pined for sympathy. Often I wept in secret, wishing I had gone West, to be nourished by my mother's love, instead of remaining among a cold race whose hearts were frozen hard with prejudice.

During the fall and winter seasons I scarcely had a real friend, though by that time several of my classmates were courteous to me at a safe distance.

My mother had not yet forgiven my rudeness to her, and I had no moment for letter-writing. By daylight and lamplight, I spun with reeds and thistles, until my hands were tired from their weaving, the magic design which promised me the white man's respect.

At length, in the spring term, I entered an oratorical contest among the various classes. As the day of competition approached, it did not seem possible that the event was so near at hand, but it came. In the chapel the classes assembled together, with their invited guests. The high platform was carpeted, and gayly festooned with college colors. A bright white light illumined the room, and outlined clearly the great polished beams that arched the domed ceiling. The assembled crowds filled the air with pulsating murmurs. When the hour for speaking arrived all were hushed. But on the wall the old clock which pointed out the trying moment ticked calmly on.

One after another I saw and heard the orators. Still, I could not realize that they longed for the favorable decision of the judges as much as I did. Each contestant received a loud burst of applause, and some were cheered heartily. Too soon my turn came, and I paused a moment behind the curtains for a deep breath. After my concluding words, I heard the same applause that the others had called out.

Upon my retreating steps, I was astounded to receive from my fellow-students a large bouquet of roses tied with flowing ribbons. With the lovely flowers I fled from the stage. This friendly token was a rebuke to me for the hard feelings I had borne them.

Later, the decision of the judges awarded me the first place. Then there was a mad uproar in the hall, where my classmates sang and shouted my name at the top of their lungs; and the disappointed students howled and brayed in fearfully dissonant tin trumpets. In this excitement, happy students rushed forward to offer their congratulations. And I could not conceal a smile when they wished to escort me in a procession to the students' parlor, where all were going to calm themselves. Thanking them for the kind spirit which prompted them to make such a proposition, I walked alone with the night to my own little room.

A few weeks afterward, I appeared as the college representative in another contest. This time the competition was among orators from different colleges in our State. It was held at the State capital, in one of the largest opera houses.

Here again was a strong prejudice against my people. In the evening, as the great audience filled the house, the student bodies began warring among themselves. Fortunately, I was spared witnessing any of the noisy wrangling before the contest began. The slurs against the Indian that stained the lips of our opponents were already burning like a dry fever within my breast.

But after the orations were delivered a deeper burn awaited me. There, before that vast ocean of eyes, some college rowdies threw out a large white flag, with a drawing of a most forlorn Indian girl on it. Under this they had printed in bold black letters words that ridiculed the college which was represented by a "squaw." Such worse than barbarian rudeness embittered me. While we waited for the verdict of the judges, I gleamed fiercely upon the throngs of palefaces. My teeth were hard set, as I saw the white flag still floating insolently in the air.

Then anxiously we watched the man carry toward the stage the envelope containing the final decision.

There were two prizes given, that night, and one of them was mine!

The evil spirit laughed within me when the white flag dropped out of sight, and the hands which furled it hung limp in defeat.

Leaving the crowd as quickly as possible, I was soon in my room. The rest of the night I sat in an armchair and gazed into the crackling fire. I laughed no more in triumph when thus alone. The little taste of victory did not satisfy a hunger in my heart. In my mind I saw my mother far away on the Western plains, and she was holding a charge against me.

# AN INDIAN TEACHER
# AMONG INDIANS

## I.
## MY FIRST DAY

THOUGH AN ILLNESS left me unable to continue my college course, my pride kept me from returning to my mother. Had she known of my worn condition, she would have said the white man's papers were not worth the freedom and health I had lost by them. Such a rebuke from my mother would have been unbearable, and as I felt then it would be far too true to be comfortable.

Since the winter when I had my first dreams about red apples I had been traveling slowly toward the morning horizon. There had been no doubt about the direction in which I wished to go to spend my energies in a work for the Indian race. Thus I had written my mother briefly, saying my plan for the year was to teach in an Eastern Indian school. Sending this message to her in the West, I started at once eastward.

Thus I found myself, tired and hot, in a black veiling of car smoke, as I stood wearily on a street corner of an old-fashioned town, waiting for a car. In a few moments more I should be on the school grounds, where a new work was ready for my inexperienced hands.

Upon entering the school campus, I was surprised at the thickly clustered buildings which made it a quaint little village, much more interesting than the town itself. The large trees among the houses gave the place a cool, refreshing shade, and the grass a deeper green. Within this large court of grass and trees stood a low green pump. The queer boxlike case had a revolving handle on its side, which clanked and creaked constantly.

I made myself known and was shown to my room,—a small, carpeted room, with ghastly walls and ceiling. The two windows, both on the same side, were curtained with heavy muslin yellowed with age. A clean white bed was in one corner of the room, and opposite it was a square pine table covered with a black woolen blanket.

Without removing my hat from my head, I seated myself in one of the two stiff-backed chairs that were placed beside the table. For several heart throbs I sat still looking from ceiling to floor, from wall to wall, trying hard to imagine years of contentment there. Even while I was wondering if my exhausted strength would sustain me through this undertaking, I heard a heavy tread stop at my door. Opening it, I met the imposing figure of a stately gray-haired man. With a light straw hat in one hand, and the right hand extended for greeting, he smiled kindly upon me. For some reason I was awed by his wondrous height and his strong square shoulders, which I felt were a finger's length above my head.

I was always slight, and my serious illness in the early spring had made me look rather frail and languid. His quick eye measured my height and breadth. Then he looked into my face. I imagined that a visible shadow flitted across his countenance as he let my hand fall. I knew he was no other than my employer.

"Ah ha! so you are the little Indian girl who created the excitement among the college orators!" he said, more to himself than to me. I thought I heard a subtle note of disappointment in his voice. Looking in from where he stood, with one sweeping glance, he asked if I lacked anything for my room.

After he turned to go, I listened to his step until it grew faint and was lost in the distance. I was aware that my car-smoked appearance had not concealed the lines of pain on my face.

For a short moment my spirit laughed at my ill fortune, and I entertained the idea of exerting myself to make an improvement. But as I tossed my hat off a leaden weakness came over me, and I felt as if years of weariness lay like water-soaked logs upon me. I threw myself upon the bed, and, closing my eyes, forgot my good intention.

## II.
## A TRIP WESTWARD

One sultry month I sat at a desk heaped up with work. Now, as I recall it, I wonder how I could have dared to disregard nature's warning with such recklessness. Fortunately, my inheritance of a marvelous endurance enabled me to bend without breaking.

Though I had gone to and fro, from my room to the office, in an unhappy silence, I was watched by those around me. On an early morning I was summoned to the superintendent's office. For a half-hour I listened to his words, and when I returned to my room I remembered one sentence above the rest. It was this: "I am going to turn you loose to pasture!" He was sending me West to gather Indian pupils for the school, and this was his way of expressing it.

I needed nourishment, but the mid-summer's travel across the continent to search the hot prairies for overconfident parents who would intrust their children to strangers was a lean pasturage. However, I dwelt on the hope of seeing my mother. I tried to reason that a change was a rest. Within a couple of days I started toward my mother's home.

The intense heat and the sticky car smoke that followed my homeward trail did not noticeably restore my vitality. Hour after hour I gazed upon the country which was receding rapidly from me. I noticed the gradual expansion of the horizon as we emerged out of the forests into the plains. The great high buildings, whose towers overlooked the dense woodlands, and whose gigantic clusters formed large cities, diminished, together with the groves, until only little log cabins lay snugly in the bosom of the vast prairie. The cloud shadows which drifted about on the waving yellow of long-dried grasses thrilled me like the meeting of old friends.

At a small station, consisting of a single frame house with a rickety board walk around it, I alighted from the iron horse, just thirty miles from my mother and my brother Dawée. A strong hot wind seemed determined to blow my hat off, and return me to olden days when I roamed bareheaded over the hills. After the puffing engine of my train was gone, I stood on the platform in deep solitude. In the distance I saw the gently rolling land leap up into bare hills. At their bases a broad gray road was winding itself round about them until it came by the station. Among these hills I rode in a light conveyance, with a trusty driver, whose unkempt flaxen hair hung shaggy about his ears and his leather neck of reddish tan. From accident or decay he had lost one of his long front teeth.

Though I call him a paleface, his cheeks were of a brick red. His moist blue eyes, blurred and bloodshot, twitched involuntarily. For a long time he had driven through grass and snow from this solitary station to the Indian village. His weather-stained clothes fitted badly his warped shoulders. He was stooped, and his protruding chin, with its tuft of dry flax, nodded as monotonously as did the head of his faithful beast.

All the morning I looked about me, recognizing old familiar sky lines of rugged bluffs and round-topped hills. By the roadside I caught glimpses of various plants whose sweet roots were delicacies among my people. When I saw the first cone-shaped wigwam, I could not help uttering an exclamation which caused my driver a sudden jump out of his drowsy nodding.

At noon, as we drove through the eastern edge of the reservation, I grew very impatient and restless. Constantly I wondered what my mother would say upon seeing her little daughter grown tall. I had not written her the day of my arrival, thinking I would surprise her. Crossing a ravine thicketed with low shrubs and plum bushes, we approached a large yellow acre of wild sunflowers. Just beyond this nature's garden we drew near to my mother's cottage. Close by the log cabin stood a little canvas-covered wigwam. The driver stopped in front of the open door, and in a long moment my mother appeared at the threshold.

I had expected her to run out to greet me, but she stood still, all the while staring at the weather-beaten man at my side. At length, when her loftiness became unbearable, I called to her, "Mother, why do you stop?"

This seemed to break the evil moment, and she hastened out to hold my head against her cheek.

"My daughter, what madness possessed you to bring home such a fellow?" she asked, pointing at the driver, who was fumbling in his pockets for change while he held the bill I gave him between his jagged teeth.

"Bring him! Why, no, mother, he has brought me! He is a driver!" I exclaimed.

Upon this revelation, my mother threw her arms about me and apologized for her mistaken inference. We laughed away the momentary hurt. Then she built a brisk fire on the ground in the tepee, and hung a blackened coffeepot on one of the prongs of a forked pole which leaned over the flames. Placing a pan on a heap of red embers, she baked some unleavened bread. This light luncheon she brought into the cabin, and arranged on a table covered with a checkered oilcloth.

My mother had never gone to school, and though she meant always to give up her own customs for such of the white man's ways as pleased her, she made only compromises. Her two windows, directly opposite each other, she curtained with a pink-flowered print. The naked logs were unstained, and rudely carved with the axe so as to fit into one another. The sod roof was trying to boast of tiny sunflowers, the seeds of which had probably been planted by the constant wind. As I leaned my head against the logs, I discovered the peculiar odor that I could not forget. The rains had soaked the earth and roof so that the smell of damp clay was but the natural breath of such a dwelling.

"Mother, why is not your house cemented? Do you have no interest in a more comfortable shelter?" I asked, when the apparent inconveniences of her home seemed to suggest indifference on her part.

"You forget, my child, that I am now old, and I do not work with beads any more. Your brother Dawée, too, has lost his position, and we are left without means to buy even a morsel of food," she replied.

Dawée was a government clerk in our reservation when I last heard from him. I was surprised upon hearing what my mother said concerning his lack of employment. Seeing the puzzled expression on my face, she continued: "Dawée! Oh, has he not told you that the Great Father at Washington sent a white son to take your brother's pen from him? Since then Dawée has not been able to make use of the education the Eastern school has given him."

I found no words with which to answer satisfactorily. I found no reason with which to cool my inflamed feelings.

Dawée was a whole day's journey off on the prairie, and my mother did not expect him until the next day. We were silent.

When, at length, I raised my head to hear more clearly the moaning of the wind in the corner logs, I noticed the daylight streaming into the dingy room through several places where the logs fitted unevenly. Turning to my mother, I urged her to tell me more about Dawée's trouble, but she only said: "Well, my daughter, this village has been these many winters a refuge for white robbers. The Indian cannot complain to the Great Father in Washington without suffering outrage for it here. Dawée tried to secure justice for our tribe in a small matter, and today you see the folly of it."

Again, though she stopped to hear what I might say, I was silent.

"My child, there is only one source of justice, and I have been praying steadfastly to the Great Spirit to avenge our wrongs," she said, seeing I did not move my lips.

My shattered energy was unable to hold longer any faith, and I cried out desperately: "Mother, don't pray again! The Great Spirit does not care if we live or die! Let us not look for good or justice: then we shall not be disappointed!"

"Sh! my child, do not talk so madly. There is Taku Iyotan Wasaka, to which I pray," she answered, as she stroked my head again as she used to do when I was a smaller child.

## III.
## MY MOTHER'S CURSE UPON WHITE SETTLERS

One black night mother and I sat alone in the dim starlight, in front of our wigwam. We were facing the river, as we talked about the shrinking limits of the village. She told me about the poverty-stricken white settlers, who lived in caves dug in the long ravines of the high hills across the river.

A whole tribe of broad-footed white beggars had rushed hither to make claims on those wild lands. Even as she was telling this I spied a small glimmering light in the bluffs.

"That is a white man's lodge where you see the burning fire," she said. Then, a short distance from it, only a little lower than the first, was another light. As I became accustomed to the night, I saw more and more twinkling lights, here and there, scattered all along the wide black margin of the river.

Still looking toward the distant firelight, my mother continued: "My daughter, beware of the paleface. It was the cruel paleface who caused the death of your sister and your uncle, my brave brother. It is this same paleface who offers in one palm the holy papers, and with the other gives a holy baptism of firewater. He is the hypocrite who reads with one eye, 'Thou shalt not kill,' and with the other gloats upon the sufferings of the Indian race." Then suddenly discovering a new fire in the bluffs, she exclaimed, "Well, well, my daughter, there is the light of another white rascal!"

She sprang to her feet, and, standing firm beside her wigwam, she sent a curse upon those who sat around the hated white man's light. Raising her right arm forcibly into line with her eye, she threw her whole might into her doubled fist as she shot it vehemently at the strangers. Long she held her outstretched fingers toward the settler's lodge, as if an invisible power passed from them to the evil at which she aimed.

# IV.
## RETROSPECTION

Leaving my mother, I returned to the school in the East. As months passed over me, I slowly comprehended that the large army of white teachers in Indian schools had a larger missionary creed than I had suspected.

It was one which included self-preservation quite as much as Indian education. When I saw an opium-eater holding a position as teacher of Indians, I did not understand what good was expected, until a Christian in power replied that this pumpkin-colored creature had a feeble mother to support. An inebriate paleface sat stupid in a doctor's chair, while Indian patients carried their ailments to untimely graves, because his fair wife was dependent upon him for her daily food.

I find it hard to count that white man a teacher who tortured an ambitious Indian youth by frequently reminding the brave change-ling that he was nothing but a "government pauper."

Though I burned with indignation upon discovering on every side instances no less shameful than those I have mentioned, there was no present help. Even the few rare ones who have worked nobly for my race were powerless to choose workmen like them-selves. To be sure, a man was sent from the Great Father to inspect Indian schools, but what he saw was usually the students' sample work *made* for exhibition. I was nettled by this sly cun-ning of the workmen who hoodwinked the Indian's pale Father at Washington.

My illness, which prevented the conclusion of my college course, together with my mother's stories of the encroaching fron-tier settlers, left me in no mood to strain my eyes in searching for latent good in my white co-workers.

At this stage of my own evolution, I was ready to curse men of small capacity for being the dwarfs their God had made them. In the process of my education I had lost all consciousness of the nature world about me. Thus, when a hidden rage took me to the small white-walled prison which I then called my room, I unknowingly turned away from my one salvation.

Alone in my room, I sat like the petrified Indian woman of whom my mother used to tell me. I wished my heart's burdens would turn me to unfeeling stone. But alive, in my tomb, I was destitute!

For the white man's papers I had given up my faith in the Great Spirit. For these same papers I had forgotten the healing in trees and brooks. On account of my mother's simple view of life, and my lack of any, I gave her up, also. I made no friends among the race of people I loathed. Like a slender tree, I had been uprooted from my mother, nature, and God. I was shorn of my branches, which had waved in sympathy and love for home and friends. The natural coat of bark which had protected my oversensitive nature was scraped off to the very quick.

Now a cold bare pole I seemed to be, planted in a strange earth. Still, I seemed to hope a day would come when my mute aching head, reared upward to the sky, would flash a zigzag lightning across the heavens. With this dream of vent for a long-pent consciousness, I walked again amid the crowds.

At last, one weary day in the schoolroom, a new idea presented itself to me. It was a new way of solving the problem of my inner self. I liked it. Thus I resigned my position as teacher; and now I am in an Eastern city, following the long course of study I have set for myself. Now, as I look back upon the recent past, I see it from a distance, as a whole. I remember how, from morning till evening, many specimens of civilized peoples visited the Indian school. The city folks with canes and eyeglasses, the countrymen with sunburnt cheeks and clumsy feet, forgot their relative social ranks in an ignorant curiosity. Both sorts of these Christian palefaces were alike astounded at seeing the children of savage warriors so docile and industrious.

As answers to their shallow inquiries they received the students' sample work to look upon. Examining the neatly figured pages, and gazing upon the Indian girls and boys bending over their books, the white visitors walked out of the schoolhouse well satisfied: they were educating the children of the red man! They were paying a liberal fee to the government employees in whose able hands lay the small forest of Indian timber.

In this fashion many have passed idly through the Indian schools during the last decade, afterward to boast of their charity to the North American Indian. But few there are who have paused to question whether real life or long-lasting death lies beneath this semblance of civilization.

# THE GREAT SPIRIT

WHEN THE SPIRIT swells my breast I love to roam leisurely among the green hills; or sometimes, sitting on the brink of the murmuring Missouri, I marvel at the great blue overhead. With half-closed eyes I watch the huge cloud shadows in their noiseless play upon the high bluffs opposite me, while into my ear ripple the sweet, soft cadences of the river's song. Folded hands lie in my lap, for the time forgot. My heart and I lie small upon the earth like a grain of throbbing sand. Drifting clouds and tinkling waters, together with the warmth of a genial summer day, bespeak with eloquence the loving Mystery round about us. During the idle while I sat upon the sunny river brink, I grew somewhat, though my response be not so clearly manifest as in the green grass fringing the edge of the high bluff back of me.

At length retracing the uncertain footpath scaling the precipitous embankment, I seek the level lands where grow the wild prairie flowers. And they, the lovely little folk, soothe my soul with their perfumed breath.

Their quaint round faces of varied hue convince the heart which leaps with glad surprise that they, too, are living symbols of omnipotent thought. With a child's eager eye I drink in the myriad star shapes wrought in luxuriant color upon the green. Beautiful is the spiritual essence they embody.

I leave them nodding in the breeze, but take along with me their impress upon my heart. I pause to rest me upon a rock embedded on the side of a foothill facing the low river bottom. Here the Stone-Boy, of whom the American aborigine tells, frolics about, shooting his baby arrows and shouting aloud with glee at the tiny shafts of lightning that flash from the flying arrow-beaks. What an ideal warrior he became, baffling the siege of the pests of all the land till he triumphed over their united attack. And here he lay,—Inyan our great-great-grandfather, older than the hill he rested on, older than the race of men who love to tell of his wonderful career.

Interwoven with the thread of this Indian legend of the rock, I fain would trace a subtle knowledge of the native folk which enabled them to recognize a kinship to any and all parts of this vast universe. By the leading of an ancient trail I move toward the Indian village.

With the strong, happy sense that both great and small are so surely enfolded in His magnitude that, without a miss, each has his allotted individual ground of opportunities, I am buoyant with good nature.

Yellow Breast, swaying upon the slender stem of a wild sunflower, warbles a sweet assurance of this as I pass near by. Breaking off the clear crystal song, he turns his wee head from side to side eyeing me wisely as slowly I plod with moccasined feet. Then again he yields himself to his song of joy. Flit, flit hither and yon, he fills the summer sky with his swift, sweet melody. And truly does it seem his vigorous freedom lies more in his little spirit than in his wing.

With these thoughts I reach the log cabin whither I am strongly drawn by the tie of a child to an aged mother. Out bounds my four-footed friend to meet me, frisking about my path with unmistakable delight. Chän is a black shaggy dog, "a thoroughbred little mongrel" of whom I am very fond. Chän seems to understand many words in Sioux, and will go to her mat even when I whisper the word, though generally I think she is guided by the tone of the voice. Often she tries to imitate the sliding inflection and long-drawn-out voice to the amusement of our guests, but her articulation is quite beyond my ear. In both my hands I hold her shaggy head and gaze into her large brown eyes. At once the dilated pupils contract into tiny black dots, as if the roguish spirit within would evade my questioning.

Finally resuming the chair at my desk I feel in keen sympathy with my fellow-creatures, for I seem to see clearly again that all are akin. The racial lines, which once were bitterly real, now serve nothing more than marking out a living mosaic of human beings. And even here men of the same color are like the ivory keys of one instrument where each resembles all the rest, yet varies from them in pitch and quality of voice. And those creatures who are for a time mere echoes of another's note are not unlike the fable of the thin sick man whose distorted shadow, dressed like a real creature, came to the old master to make him follow as a shadow. Thus with a compassion for all echoes in human guise, I greet the solemn-faced "native preacher" whom I find awaiting me. I listen with respect for God's creature, though he mouths most strangely the jangling phrases of a bigoted creed.

As our tribe is one large family, where every person is related to all the others, he addressed me:—

"Cousin, I came from the morning church service to talk with you."

"Yes?" I said interrogatively, as he paused for some word from me.

Shifting uneasily about in the straight-backed chair he sat upon, he began: "Every holy day (Sunday) I look about our little God's house, and not seeing you there, I am disappointed. This is why I come today. Cousin, as I watch you from afar, I see no unbecoming behavior and hear only good reports of you, which all the more burns me with the wish that you were a church member. Cousin, I was taught long years ago by kind missionaries to read the holy book. These godly men taught me also the folly of our old beliefs.

"There is one God who gives reward or punishment to the race of dead men. In the upper region the Christian dead are gathered in unceasing song and prayer. In the deep pit below, the sinful ones dance in torturing flames.

"Think upon these things, my cousin, and choose now to avoid the after-doom of hell fire!" Then followed a long silence in which he clasped tighter and unclasped again his interlocked fingers.

Like instantaneous lightning flashes came pictures of my own mother's making, for she, too, is now a follower of the new superstition.

"Knocking out the chinking of our log cabin, some evil hand thrust in a burning taper of braided dry grass, but failed of his intent, for the fire died out and the half-burned brand fell inward to the floor. Directly above it, on a shelf, lay the holy book. This is what we found after our return from a several days' visit. Surely some great power is hid in the sacred book!"

Brushing away from my eyes many like pictures, I offered midday meal to the converted Indian sitting wordless and with downcast face. No sooner had he risen from the table with "Cousin, I have relished it," than the church bell rang.

Thither he hurried forth with his afternoon sermon. I watched him as he hastened along, his eyes bent fast upon the dusty road till he disappeared at the end of a quarter of a mile.

The little incident recalled to mind the copy of a missionary paper brought to my notice a few days ago, in which a "Christian" pugilist commented upon a recent article of mine, grossly perverting the spirit of my pen. Still I would not forget that the pale-faced missionary and the hoodooed aborigine are both God's creatures, though small indeed their own conceptions of Infinite Love. A wee child toddling in a wonder world, I prefer to their dogma my excursions into the natural gardens where the voice of the Great Spirit is heard in the twittering of birds, the rippling of mighty waters, and the sweet breathing of flowers.

Here, in a fleeting quiet, I am awakened by the fluttering robe of the Great Spirit. To my innermost consciousness the phenomenal universe is a royal mantle, vibrating with His divine breath. Caught in its flowing fringes are the spangles and oscillating brilliants of sun, moon, and stars.

# THE SOFT-HEARTED SIOUX

## I.

BESIDE THE OPEN fire I sat within our tepee. With my red blanket wrapped tightly about my crossed legs, I was thinking of the coming season, my sixteenth winter. On either side of the wigwam were my parents. My father was whistling a tune between his teeth while polishing with his bare hand a red stone pipe he had recently carved. Almost in front of me, beyond the centre fire, my old grandmother sat near the entranceway.

She turned her face toward her right and addressed most of her words to my mother. Now and then she spoke to me, but never did she allow her eyes to rest upon her daughter's husband, my father. It was only upon rare occasions that my grandmother said anything to him. Thus his ears were open and ready to catch the smallest wish she might express. Sometimes when my grandmother had been saying things which pleased him, my father used to comment upon them. At other times, when he could not approve of what was spoken, he used to work or smoke silently.

On this night my old grandmother began her talk about me. Filling the bowl of her red stone pipe with dry willow bark, she looked across at me.

"My grandchild, you are tall and are no longer a little boy." Narrowing her old eyes, she asked, "My grandchild, when are you going to bring here a handsome young woman?" I stared into the fire rather than meet her gaze. Waiting for my answer, she stooped forward and through the long stem drew a flame into the red stone pipe.

I smiled while my eyes were still fixed upon the bright fire, but I said nothing in reply. Turning to my mother, she offered her the pipe. I glanced at my grandmother. The loose buckskin sleeve fell off at her elbow and showed a wrist covered with silver bracelets. Holding up the fingers of her left hand, she named off the desirable young women of our village.

"Which one, my grandchild, which one?" she questioned.

"Hoh!" I said, pulling at my blanket in confusion. "Not yet!" Here my mother passed the pipe over the fire to my father. Then she, too, began speaking of what I should do.

"My son, be always active. Do not dislike a long hunt. Learn to provide much buffalo meat and many buckskins before you bring home a wife." Presently my father gave the pipe to my grandmother, and he took his turn in the exhortations.

"Ho, my son, I have been counting in my heart the bravest warriors of our people. There is not one of them who won his title in his sixteenth winter. My son, it is a great thing for some brave of sixteen winters to do."

Not a word had I to give in answer. I knew well the fame of my warrior father. He had earned the right of speaking such words, though even he himself was a brave only at my age. Refusing to smoke my grandmother's pipe because my heart was too much stirred by their words, and sorely troubled with a fear lest I should disappoint them, I arose to go. Drawing my blanket over my shoulders, I said, as I stepped toward the entranceway: "I go to hobble my pony. It is now late in the night."

## II.

Nine winters' snows had buried deep that night when my old grandmother, together with my father and mother, designed my future with the glow of a camp fire upon it.

Yet I did not grow up the warrior, huntsman, and husband I was to have been. At the mission school I learned it was wrong to kill. Nine winters I hunted for the soft heart of Christ, and prayed for the huntsmen who chased the buffalo on the plains.

In the autumn of the tenth year I was sent back to my tribe to preach Christianity to them. With the white man's Bible in my hand, and the white man's tender heart in my breast, I returned to my own people.

Wearing a foreigner's dress, I walked, a stranger, into my father's village.

Asking my way, for I had not forgotten my native tongue, an old man led me toward the tepee where my father lay. From my old companion I learned that my father had been sick many moons. As we drew near the tepee, I heard the chanting of a medicine-man within it. At once I wished to enter in and drive from my home the sorcerer of the plains, but the old warrior checked me. "Ho, wait outside until the medicine-man leaves your father," he said. While talking he scanned me from head to feet. Then he retraced his steps toward the heart of the camping-ground.

My father's dwelling was on the outer limits of the round-faced village. With every heart-throb I grew more impatient to enter the wigwam.

While I turned the leaves of my Bible with nervous fingers, the medicine-man came forth from the dwelling and walked hurriedly away. His head and face were closely covered with the loose robe which draped his entire figure.

He was tall and large. His long strides I have never forgot. They seemed to me then the uncanny gait of eternal death. Quickly pocketing my Bible, I went into the tepee.

Upon a mat lay my father, with furrowed face and gray hair. His eyes and cheeks were sunken far into his head. His sallow skin lay thin upon his pinched nose and high cheek-bones. Stooping over him, I took his fevered hand. "How, Ate?" I greeted him. A light flashed from his listless eyes and his dried lips parted. "My son!" he murmured, in a feeble voice. Then again the wave of joy and recognition receded. He closed his eyes, and his hand dropped from my open palm to the ground.

Looking about, I saw an old woman sitting with bowed head. Shaking hands with her, I recognized my mother. I sat down between my father and mother as I used to do, but I did not feel at home. The place where my old grandmother used to sit was now unoccupied. With my mother I bowed my head. Alike our throats were choked and tears were streaming from our eyes; but far apart in spirit our ideas and faiths separated us. My grief was for the soul unsaved; and I thought my mother wept to see a brave man's body broken by sickness.

Useless was my attempt to change the faith in the medicine-man to that abstract power named God. Then one day I became righteously mad with anger that the medicine-man should thus ensnare my father's soul. And when he came to chant his sacred songs I pointed toward the door and bade him go! The man's eyes glared upon me for an instant. Slowly gathering his robe about him, he turned his back upon the sick man and stepped out of our wigwam. "Ha, ha, ha! my son, I cannot live without the medicine-man!" I heard my father cry when the sacred man was gone.

## III.

On a bright day, when the winged seeds of the prairie-grass were flying hither and thither, I walked solemnly toward the centre of the camping-ground. My heart beat hard and irregularly at my side. Tighter I grasped the sacred book I carried under my arm. Now was the beginning of life's work.

Though I knew it would be hard, I did not once feel that failure was to be my reward. As I stepped unevenly on the rolling ground, I thought of the warriors soon to wash off their war-paints and follow me.

At length I reached the place where the people had assembled to hear me preach. In a large circle men and women sat upon the dry red grass. Within the ring I stood, with the white man's Bible in my hand. I tried to tell them of the soft heart of Christ.

In silence the vast circle of bareheaded warriors sat under an afternoon sun. At last, wiping the wet from my brow, I took my place in the ring. The hush of the assembly filled me with great hope.

I was turning my thoughts upward to the sky in gratitude, when a stir called me to earth again.

A tall, strong man arose. His loose robe hung in folds over his right shoulder. A pair of snapping black eyes fastened themselves like the poisonous fangs of a serpent upon me. He was the medicine-man. A tremor played about my heart and a chill cooled the fire in my veins.

Scornfully he pointed a long forefinger in my direction and asked, "What loyal son is he who, returning to his father's people, wears a foreigner's dress?" He paused a moment, and then continued: "The dress of that foreigner of whom a story says he bound a native of our land, and heaping dry sticks around him, kindled a fire at his feet!" Waving his hand toward me, he exclaimed, "Here is the traitor to his people!"

I was helpless. Before the eyes of the crowd the cunning magician turned my honest heart into a vile nest of treachery. Alas! the people frowned as they looked upon me.

"Listen!" he went on. "Which one of you who have eyed the young man can see through his bosom and warn the people of the nest of young snakes hatching there? Whose ear was so acute that he caught the hissing of snakes whenever the young man opened his mouth? This one has not only proven false to you, but even to the Great Spirit who made him. He is a fool! Why do you sit here giving ear to a foolish man who could not defend his people because he fears to kill, who could not bring venison to renew the life of his sick father? With his prayers, let him drive away the enemy! With his soft heart, let him keep off starvation! We shall go elsewhere to dwell upon an untainted ground."

With this he disbanded the people. When the sun lowered in the west and the winds were quiet, the village of cone-shaped tepees was gone. The medicine-man had won the hearts of the people.

Only my father's dwelling was left to mark the fighting-ground.

## IV.

From a long night at my father's bedside I came out to look upon the morning. The yellow sun hung equally between the snow-covered land and the cloudless blue sky. The light of the new day was cold. The strong breath of winter crusted the snow and fitted crystal shells over the rivers and lakes. As I stood in front of the tepee, thinking of the vast prairies which separated us from our tribe, and wondering if the high sky likewise separated the soft-hearted Son of God from us, the icy blast from the North blew through my hair and skull. My neglected hair had grown long and fell upon my neck.

My father had not risen from his bed since the day the medicine-man led the people away. Though I read from the Bible and prayed beside him upon my knees, my father would not listen. Yet I believed my prayers were not unheeded in heaven.

"Ha, ha, ha! my son," my father groaned upon the first snow-fall. "My son, our food is gone. There is no one to bring me meat! My son, your soft heart has unfitted you for everything!" Then covering his face with the buffalo-robe, he said no more. Now while I stood out in that cold winter morning, I was starving. For two days I had not seen any food. But my own cold and hunger did not harass my soul as did the whining cry of the sick old man.

Stepping again into the tepee, I untied my snow-shoes, which were fastened to the tent-poles.

My poor mother, watching by the sick one, and faithfully heaping wood upon the centre fire, spoke to me:

"My son, do not fail again to bring your father meat, or he will starve to death."

"How, Ina," I answered, sorrowfully. From the tepee I started forth again to hunt food for my aged parents. All day I tracked the white level lands in vain. Nowhere, nowhere were there any other footprints but my own! In the evening of this third fast-day I came back without meat. Only a bundle of sticks for the fire I brought on my back. Dropping the wood outside, I lifted the door-flap and set one foot within the tepee.

There I grew dizzy and numb. My eyes swam in tears. Before me lay my old gray-haired father sobbing like a child. In his horny hands he clutched the buffalo-robe, and with his teeth he was gnawing off the edges. Chewing the dry stiff hair and buffalo-skin, my father's eyes sought my hands. Upon seeing them empty, he cried out:

"My son, your soft heart will let me starve before you bring me meat! Two hills eastward stand a herd of cattle. Yet you will see me die before you bring me food!"

Leaving my mother lying with covered head upon her mat, I rushed out into the night.

With a strange warmth in my heart and swiftness in my feet, I climbed over the first hill, and soon the second one. The moonlight upon the white country showed me a clear path to the white man's cattle. With my hand upon the knife in my belt, I leaned heavily against the fence while counting the herd.

Twenty in all I numbered. From among them I chose the best-fattened creature. Leaping over the fence, I plunged my knife into it.

My long knife was sharp, and my hands, no more fearful and slow, slashed off choice chunks of warm flesh. Bending under the meat I had taken for my starving father, I hurried across the prairie.

Toward home I fairly ran with the life-giving food I carried upon my back. Hardly had I climbed the second hill when I heard sounds coming after me. Faster and faster I ran with my load for my father, but the sounds were gaining upon me. I heard the clicking of snowshoes and the squeaking of the leather straps at my heels; yet I did not turn to see what pursued me, for I was intent upon reaching my father. Suddenly like thunder an angry voice shouted curses and threats into my ear! A rough hand wrenched my shoulder and took the meat from me! I stopped struggling to run. A deafening whir filled my head. The moon and stars began to move. Now the white prairie was sky, and the stars lay under my feet. Now again they were turning. At last the starry blue rose up into place. The noise in my ears was still. A great quiet filled the air. In my hand I found my long knife dripping with blood. At my feet a man's figure lay prone in blood-red snow. The horrible scene about me seemed a trick of my senses, for I could not understand it was real. Looking long upon the blood-stained snow, the load of meat for my starving father reached my recognition at last. Quickly I tossed it over my shoulder and started again homeward.

Tired and haunted I reached the door of the wigwam. Carrying the food before me, I entered with it into the tepee.

"Father, here is food!" I cried, as I dropped the meat near my mother. No answer came. Turning about, I beheld my gray-haired father dead! I saw by the unsteady firelight an old gray-haired skeleton lying rigid and stiff.

Out into the open I started, but the snow at my feet became bloody.

## V.

On the day after my father's death, having led my mother to the camp of the medicine-man, I gave myself up to those who were searching for the murderer of the paleface.

They bound me hand and foot. Here in this cell I was placed four days ago.

The shrieking winter winds have followed me hither. Rattling the bars, they howl unceasingly: "Your soft heart! your soft heart will see me die before you bring me food!" Hark! something is clanking the chain on the door. It is being opened. From the dark night without a black figure crosses the threshold. ★ ★ ★ It is the guard. He comes to warn me of my fate. He tells me that tomorrow I must die. In his stern face I laugh aloud. I do not fear death.

Yet I wonder who shall come to welcome me in the realm of strange sight. Will the loving Jesus grant me pardon and give my soul a soothing sleep? or will my warrior father greet me and receive me as his son? Will my spirit fly upward to a happy heaven?

or shall I sink into the bottomless pit, an outcast from a God of infinite love?

Soon, soon I shall know, for now I see the east is growing red. My heart is strong. My face is calm. My eyes are dry and eager for new scenes. My hands hang quietly at my side. Serene and brave, my soul awaits the men to perch me on the gallows for another flight. I go.

# THE TRIAL PATH

It was an autumn night on the plain. The smoke-lapels of the cone-shaped tepee flapped gently in the breeze. From the low night sky, with its myriad fire points, a large bright star peeped in at the smoke-hole of the wigwam between its fluttering lapels, down upon two Dakotas talking in the dark. The mellow stream from the star above, a maid of twenty summers, on a bed of sweet-grass, drank in with her wakeful eyes. On the opposite side of the tepee, beyond the centre fireplace, the grandmother spread her rug. Though once she had lain down, the telling of a story has aroused her to a sitting posture.

Her eyes are tight closed. With a thin palm she strokes her wind-shorn hair.

"Yes, my grandchild, the legend says the large bright stars are wise old warriors, and the small dim ones are handsome young braves," she reiterates, in a high, tremulous voice.

"Then this one peeping in at the smoke-hole yonder is my dear old grandfather," muses the young woman, in long-drawn-out words.

Her soft rich voice floats through the darkness within the tepee, over the cold ashes heaped on the centre fire, and passes into the ear of the toothless old woman, who sits dumb in silent reverie. Thence it flies on swifter wing over many winter snows, till at last it cleaves the warm light atmosphere of her grandfather's youth. From there her grandmother made answer:

"Listen! I am young again. It is the day of your grandfather's death. The elder one, I mean, for there were two of them. They were like twins, though they were not brothers. They were friends, inseparable! All things, good and bad, they shared together, save one, which made them mad. In that heated frenzy the younger man slew his most intimate friend. He killed his elder brother, for long had their affection made them kin."

The voice of the old woman broke. Swaying her stooped shoulders to and fro as she sat upon her feet, she muttered vain exclamations beneath her breath. Her eyes, closed tight against the night, beheld behind them the light of bygone days. They saw again a rolling black cloud spread itself over the land. Her ear heard the deep rumbling of a tempest in the west. She bent low a cowering head, while angry thunder-birds shrieked across the sky. "Heyä! heyä!" (No! no!) groaned the toothless grandmother at the fury she had awakened. But the glorious peace afterward, when yellow sunshine made the people glad, now lured her memory onward through the storm.

"How fast, how loud my heart beats as I listen to the messenger's horrible tale!" she ejaculates. "From the fresh grave of the murdered man he hurried to our wigwam. Deliberately crossing his bare shins, he sat down unbidden beside my father, smoking a long-stemmed pipe. He had scarce caught his breath when, panting, he began:

"'He was an only son, and a much-adored brother.'

"With wild, suspecting eyes he glanced at me as if I were in league with the man-killer, my lover. My father, exhaling sweet-scented smoke, assented—'How.' Then interrupting the 'Eya' on the lips of the round-eyed tale-bearer, he asked, 'My friend, will you smoke?' He took the pipe by its red-stone bowl, and pointed the long slender stem toward the man. 'Yes, yes, my friend,' replied he, and reached out a long brown arm.

"For many heart-throbs he puffed out the blue smoke, which hung like a cloud between us. But even through the smoke-mist I saw his sharp black eyes glittering toward me. I longed to ask what doom awaited the young murderer, but dared not open my lips, lest I burst forth into screams instead. My father plied the question. Returning the pipe, the man replied: 'Oh, the chieftain and his chosen men have had counsel together. They have agreed it is not safe to allow a man-killer loose in our midst. He who kills one of our tribe is an enemy, and must suffer the fate of a foe.'

"My temples throbbed like a pair of hearts!

"While I listened, a crier passed by my father's tepee. Mounted, and swaying with his pony's steps, he proclaimed in a loud voice these words (hark! I hear them now!): "Ho-po! Give ear, all you people. A terrible deed is done. Two friends—ay, brothers in heart—have quarreled together. Now one lies buried on the hill, while the other sits, a dreaded man-killer, within his dwelling." Says our chieftain: "He who kills one of our tribe commits the offence of an enemy. As such he must be tried. Let the father of the dead man choose the mode of torture or taking of life. He has suffered livid pain, and he alone can judge how great the punishment must be to avenge his wrong." It is done.

" 'Come, every one, to witness the judgment of a father upon him who was once his son's best friend. A wild pony is now lassoed. The man-killer must mount and ride the ranting beast. Stand you all in two parallel lines from the centre tepee of the bereaved family to the wigwam opposite in the great outer ring. Between you, in the wide space, is the given trialway. From the outer circle the rider must mount and guide his pony toward the centre tepee. If, having gone the entire distance, the man-killer gains the centre tepee, still sitting on the pony's back, his life is spared and pardon given. But should he fall, then he himself has chosen death.'

"The crier's words now cease. A lull holds the village breathless. Then hurrying feet tear along, swish, swish, through the tall grass. Sobbing women hasten toward the trialway. The muffled groan of the round camp-ground is unbearable. With my face hid in the folds of my blanket, I run with the crowd toward the open place in the outer circle of our village. In a moment the two long files of solemn-faced people mark the path of the public trial. Ah! I see strong men trying to lead the lassoed pony, pitching and rearing, with white foam flying from his mouth. I choke with pain as I recognize my handsome lover desolately alone, striding with set face toward the lassoed pony. 'Do not fall! Choose life and me!' I cry in my breast, but over my lips I hold my thick blanket.

"In an instant he has leaped astride the frightened beast, and the men have let go their hold. Like an arrow sprung from a strong bow, the pony, with extended nostrils, plunges halfway to the centre tepee. With all his might the rider draws the strong reins in. The pony halts with wooden legs. The rider is thrown forward by force, but does not fall. Now the maddened creature pitches, with flying heels. The line of men and women sways outward. Now it is back in place, safe from the kicking, snorting thing.

"The pony is fierce, with its large black eyes bulging out of their sockets. With humped back and nose to the ground, it leaps into the air. I shut my eyes. I cannot see him fall.

"A loud shout goes up from the hoarse throats of men and women. I look. So! The wild horse is conquered. My lover dismounts at the doorway of the centre wigwam. The pony, wet with sweat and shaking with exhaustion, stands like a guilty dog at his master's side. Here at the entranceway of the tepee sit the bereaved father, mother, and sister. The old warrior father rises. Stepping forward two long strides, he grasps the hand of the murderer of his only son. Holding it so the people can see, he cries, with compassionate voice, 'My son!' A murmur of surprise sweeps like a puff of sudden wind along the lines.

"The mother, with swollen eyes, with her hair cut square with her shoulders, now rises. Hurrying to the young man, she takes his right hand. 'My son!' she greets him. But on the second word her voice shook, and she turned away in sobs.

"The young people rivet their eyes upon the young woman. She does not stir. With bowed head, she sits motionless. The old warrior speaks to her. 'Shake hands with the young brave, my little daughter. He was your brother's friend for many years. Now he must be both friend and brother to you.'

"Hereupon the girl rises. Slowly reaching out her slender hand, she cries, with twitching lips, 'My brother!' The trial ends."

"Grandmother!" exploded the girl on the bed of sweet-grass. "Is this true?"

"Tosh!" answered the grandmother, with a warmth in her voice. "It is all true. During the fifteen winters of our wedded life many ponies passed from our hands, but this little winner, Ohiyesa, was a constant member of our family. At length, on that sad day your grandfather died, Ohiyesa was killed at the grave."

Though the various groups of stars which move across the sky, marking the passing of time, told how the night was in its zenith, the old Dakota woman ventured an explanation of the burial ceremony.

"My grandchild, I have scarce ever breathed the sacred knowledge in my heart. Tonight I must tell you one of them. Surely you are old enough to understand.

"Our wise medicine-man said I did well to hasten Ohiyesa after his master. Perchance on the journey along the ghostpath your grandfather will weary, and in his heart wish for his pony. The creature, already bound on the spirit-trail, will be drawn by that subtle wish. Together master and beast will enter the next camp-ground."

The woman ceased her talking. But only the deep breathing of the girl broke the quiet, for now the night wind had lulled itself to sleep.

"Hinnu! hinnu! Asleep! I have been talking in the dark, unheard. I did wish the girl would plant in her heart this sacred tale," muttered she, in a querulous voice.

Nestling into her bed of sweet-scented grass, she dozed away into another dream. Still the guardian star in the night sky beamed compassionately down upon the little tepee on the plain.

# A WARRIOR'S DAUGHTER

IN THE AFTERNOON shadow of a large tepee, with red-painted smoke lapels, sat a warrior father with crossed shins. His head was so poised that his eye swept easily the vast level land to the eastern horizon line.

He was the chieftain's bravest warrior. He had won by heroic deeds the privilege of staking his wigwam within the great circle of tepees.

He was also one of the most generous gift givers to the toothless old people. For this he was entitled to the red-painted smoke lapels on his cone-shaped dwelling. He was proud of his honors. He never wearied of rehearsing nightly his own brave deeds. Though by wigwam fires he prated much of his high rank and widespread fame, his great joy was a wee black-eyed daughter of eight sturdy winters. Thus as he sat upon the soft grass, with his wife at his side, bent over her bead work, he was singing a dance song, and beat lightly the rhythm with his slender hands.

His shrewd eyes softened with pleasure as he watched the easy movements of the small body dancing on the green before him.

Tusee is taking her first dancing lesson. Her tightly-braided hair curves over both brown ears like a pair of crooked little horns which glisten in the summer sun.

With her snugly moccasined feet close together, and a wee hand at her belt to stay the long string of beads which hang from her bare neck, she bends her knees gently to the rhythm of her father's voice.

Now she ventures upon the earnest movement, slightly upward and sidewise, in a circle. At length the song drops into a closing cadence, and the little woman, clad in beaded deerskin, sits down beside the elder one. Like her mother, she sits upon her feet. In a

59

brief moment the warrior repeats the last refrain. Again Tusee springs to her feet and dances to the swing of the few final measures.

Just as the dance was finished, an elderly man, with short, thick hair loose about his square shoulders, rode into their presence from the rear, and leaped lightly from his pony's back. Dropping the rawhide rein to the ground, he tossed himself lazily on the grass. "Hunhe, you have returned soon," said the warrior, while extending a hand to his little daughter.

Quickly the child ran to her father's side and cuddled close to him, while he tenderly placed a strong arm about her. Both father and child, eyeing the figure on the grass, waited to hear the man's report.

"It is true," began the man, with a stranger's accent. "This is the night of the dance."

"Hunha!" muttered the warrior with some surprise.

Propping himself upon his elbows, the man raised his face. His features were of the Southern type. From an enemy's camp he was taken captive long years ago by Tusee's father. But the unusual qualities of the slave had won the Sioux warrior's heart, and for the last three winters the man had had his freedom. He was made real man again. His hair was allowed to grow. However, he himself had chosen to stay in the warrior's family.

"Hunha!" again ejaculated the warrior father. Then turning to his little daughter, he asked, "Tusee, do you hear that?"

"Yes, father, and I am going to dance tonight!"

With these words she bounded out of his arm and frolicked about in glee. Hereupon the proud mother's voice rang out in a chiding laugh.

"My child, in honor of your first dance your father must give a generous gift. His ponies are wild, and roam beyond the great hill. Pray, what has he fit to offer?" she questioned, the pair of puzzled eyes fixed upon her.

"A pony from the herd, mother, a fleet-footed pony from the herd!" Tusee shouted with sudden inspiration.

Pointing a small forefinger toward the man lying on the grass, she cried, "Uncle, you will go after the pony tomorrow!" And pleased with her solution of the problem, she skipped wildly about. Her childish faith in her elders was not conditioned by a knowledge of human limitations, but thought all things possible to grown-ups.

"Hähob!" exclaimed the mother, with a rising inflection, implying by the expletive that her child's buoyant spirit be not weighted with a denial.

Quickly to the hard request the man replied, "How! I go if Tusee tells me so!"

This delighted the little one, whose black eyes brimmed over with light. Standing in front of the strong man, she clapped her small, brown hands with joy.

"That makes me glad! My heart is good! Go, uncle, and bring a handsome pony!" she cried. In an instant she would have frisked away, but an impulse held her tilting where she stood. In the man's own tongue, for he had taught her many words and phrases, she exploded, "Thank you, good uncle, thank you!" then tore away from sheer excess of glee.

The proud warrior father, smiling and narrowing his eyes, muttered approval, "Howo! Hechetu!"

Like her mother, Tusee has finely pencilled eyebrows and slightly extended nostrils; but in her sturdiness of form she resembles her father.

A loyal daughter, she sits within her tepee making beaded deerskins for her father, while he longs to stave off her every suitor as all unworthy of his old heart's pride. But Tusee is not alone in her dwelling. Near the entrance-way a young brave is half reclining on a mat. In silence he watches the petals of a wild rose growing on the soft buckskin. Quickly the young woman slips the beads on the silvery sinew thread, and works them into the pretty flower design. Finally, in a low, deep voice, the young man begins:

"The sun is far past the zenith. It is now only a man's height above the western edge of land. I hurried hither to tell you tomorrow I join the war party."

He pauses for reply, but the maid's head drops lower over her deerskin, and her lips are more firmly drawn together. He continues:

"Last night in the moonlight I met your warrior father. He seemed to know I had just stepped forth from your tepee. I fear he did not like it, for though I greeted him, he was silent. I halted in his pathway. With what boldness I dared, while my heart was beating hard and fast, I asked him for his only daughter.

"Drawing himself erect to his tallest height, and gathering his loose robe more closely about his proud figure, he flashed a pair of piercing eyes upon me.

" 'Young man,' said he, with a cold, slow voice that chilled me to the marrow of my bones, 'hear me. Naught but an enemy's scalp-lock, plucked fresh with your own hand, will buy Tusee for your wife.' Then he turned on his heel and stalked away."

Tusee thrusts her work aside. With earnest eyes she scans her lover's face.

"My father's heart is really kind. He would know if you are brave and true," murmured the daughter, who wished no ill-will between her two loved ones.

Then rising to go, the youth holds out a right hand. "Grasp my hand once firmly before I go, Hoye. Pray tell me, will you wait and watch for my return?"

Tusee only nods assent, for mere words are vain.

At early dawn the round camp-ground awakes into song. Men and women sing of bravery and of triumph. They inspire the swelling breasts of the painted warriors mounted on prancing ponies bedecked with the green branches of trees.

Riding slowly around the great ring of cone-shaped tepees, here and there, a loud-singing warrior swears to avenge a former wrong, and thrusts a bare brown arm against the purple east, calling the Great Spirit to hear his vow. All having made the circuit, the singing war party gallops away southward.

Astride their ponies laden with food and deerskins, brave elderly women follow after their warriors. Among the foremost rides a young woman in elaborately beaded buckskin dress. Proudly mounted, she curbs with the single rawhide loop a wild-eyed pony.

It is Tusee on her father's warhorse. Thus the war party of Indian men and their faithful women vanish beyond the southern skyline.

A day's journey brings them very near the enemy's borderland. Nightfall finds a pair of twin tepees nestled in a deep ravine. Within one lounge the painted warriors, smoking their pipes and telling weird stories by the firelight, while in the other watchful women crouch uneasily about their center fire.

By the first gray light in the east the tepees are banished. They are gone. The warriors are in the enemy's camp, breaking dreams with their tomahawks. The women are hid away in secret places in the long thicketed ravine.

The day is far spent, the red sun is low over the west.

At length straggling warriors return, one by one, to the deep hollow. In the twilight they number their men. Three are missing.

Of these absent ones two are dead; but the third one, a young man, is a captive to the foe.

"He-he!" lament the warriors, taking food in haste.

In silence each woman, with long strides, hurries to and fro, tying large bundles on her pony's back. Under cover of night the war party must hasten homeward. Motionless, with bowed head, sits a woman in her hiding-place. She grieves for her lover.

In bitterness of spirit she hears the warriors' murmuring words. With set teeth she plans to cheat the hated enemy of their captive. In the meanwhile low signals are given, and the war party, unaware of Tusee's absence, steal quietly away. The soft thud of pony-hoofs grows fainter and fainter. The gradual hush of the empty ravine whirrs noisily in the ear of the young woman. Alert for any sound of footfalls nigh, she holds her breath to listen. Her right hand rests on a long knife in her belt. Ah, yes, she knows where her pony is hid, but not yet has she need of him. Satisfied that no danger is nigh, she prowls forth from her place of hiding. With a panther's tread and pace she climbs the high ridge beyond the low ravine. From thence she spies the enemy's camp-fires.

Rooted to the barren bluff the slender woman's figure stands on the pinnacle of night, outlined against a starry sky. The cool night breeze wafts to her burning ear snatches of song and drum. With desperate hate she bites her teeth.

Tusee beckons the stars to witness. With impassioned voice and uplifted face she pleads:

"Great Spirit, speed me to my lover's rescue! Give me swift cunning for a weapon this night! All-powerful Spirit, grant me my warrior-father's heart, strong to slay a foe and mighty to save a friend!"

In the midst of the enemy's camp-ground, underneath a temporary dance-house, are men and women in gala-day dress. It is late in the night, but the merry warriors bend and bow their nude, painted bodies before a bright center fire. To the lusty men's voices and the rhythmic throbbing drum, they leap and rebound with feathered headgears waving.

Women with red-painted cheeks and long, braided hair sit in a large half-circle against the willow railing. They, too, join in the singing, and rise to dance with their victorious warriors.

Amid this circular dance arena stands a prisoner bound to a post, haggard with shame and sorrow. He hangs his disheveled head.

He stares with unseeing eyes upon the bare earth at his feet. With jeers and smirking faces the dancers mock the Dakota captive. Rowdy braves and small boys hoot and yell in derision.

Silent among the noisy mob, a tall woman, leaning both elbows on the round willow railing, peers into the lighted arena. The dancing center fire shines bright into her handsome face, intensifying the night in her dark eyes. It breaks into myriad points upon her beaded dress. Unmindful of the surging throng jostling her at either side, she glares in upon the hateful, scoffing men. Suddenly she turns her head. Tittering maids whisper near her ear:

"There! There! See him now, sneering in the captive's face. 'Tis he who sprang upon the young man and dragged him by his long hair to yonder post. See! He is handsome! How gracefully he dances!"

The silent young woman looks toward the bound captive. She sees a warrior, scarce older than the captive, flourishing a tomahawk in the Dakota's face. A burning rage darts forth from her eyes and brands him for a victim of revenge. Her heart mutters within her breast, "Come, I wish to meet you, vile foe, who captured my lover and tortures him now with a living death."

Here the singers hush their voices, and the dancers scatter to their various resting-places along the willow ring. The victor gives a reluctant last twirl of his tomahawk, then, like the others, he leaves the center ground. With head and shoulders swaying from side to side, he carries a high-pointing chin toward the willow railing. Sitting down upon the ground with crossed legs, he fans himself with an outspread turkey wing.

Now and then he stops his haughty blinking to peep out of the corners of his eyes. He hears some one clearing her throat gently. It is unmistakably for his ear. The wing-fan swings irregularly to and fro. At length he turns a proud face over a bare shoulder and beholds a handsome woman smiling.

"Ah, she would speak to a hero!" thumps his heart wildly.

The singers raise their voices in unison. The music is irresistible. Again lunges the victor into the open arena. Again he leers into the captive's face. At every interval between the songs he returns to his resting-place. Here the young woman awaits him. As he approaches she smiles boldly into his eyes. He is pleased with her face and her smile.

Waving his wing-fan spasmodically in front of his face, he sits with his ears pricked up. He catches a low whisper. A hand taps him lightly on the shoulder. The handsome woman speaks to him in his own tongue. "Come out into the night. I wish to tell you who I am."

He must know what sweet words of praise the handsome woman has for him. With both hands he spreads the meshes of the loosely-woven willows, and crawls out unnoticed into the dark.

Before him stands the young woman. Beckoning him with a slender hand, she steps backward, away from the light and the restless throng of onlookers. He follows with impatient strides. She quickens her pace. He lengthens his strides. Then suddenly the woman turns from him and darts away with amazing speed. Clinching his fists and biting his lower lip, the young man runs after the fleeing woman. In his maddened pursuit he forgets the dance arena.

Beside a cluster of low bushes the woman halts. The young man, panting for breath and plunging headlong forward, whispers loud, "Pray tell me, are you a woman or an evil spirit to lure me away?"

Turning on heels firmly planted in the earth, the woman gives a wild spring forward, like a panther for its prey. In a husky voice she hissed between her teeth, "I am a Dakota woman!"

From her unerring long knife the enemy falls heavily at her feet. The Great Spirit heard Tusee's prayer on the hilltop. He gave her a warrior's strong heart to lessen the foe by one.

A bent old woman's figure, with a bundle like a grandchild slung on her back, walks round and round the dance-house. The wearied onlookers are leaving in twos and threes. The tired dancers creep out of the willow railing, and some go out at the entrance way, till the singers, too, rise from the drum and are trudging drowsily homeward. Within the arena the center fire lies broken in red embers. The night no longer lingers about the willow railing, but, hovering into the dance-house, covers here and there a snoring man whom sleep has overpowered where he sat.

The captive in his tight-binding rawhide ropes hangs in hopeless despair. Close about him the gloom of night is slowly crouching. Yet the last red, crackling embers cast a faint light upon his long black hair, and, shining through the thick mats, caress his wan face with undying hope.

Still about the dance-house the old woman prowls. Now the embers are gray with ashes.

The old bent woman appears at the entrance way. With a cautious, groping foot she enters. Whispering between her teeth a lullaby for her sleeping child in her blanket, she searches for something forgotten.

Noisily snored the dreaming men in the darkest parts. As the lisping old woman draws nigh, the captive again opens his eyes.

A forefinger she presses to her lip. The young man arouses himself from his stupor. His senses belie him. Before his wide-open eyes the old bent figure straightens into its youthful stature. Tusee herself is beside him. With a stroke upward and downward she severs the cruel cords with her sharp blade. Dropping her blanket from her shoulders, so that it hangs from her girdled waist like a skirt, she shakes the large bundle into a light shawl for her lover. Quickly she spreads it over his bare back.

"Come!" she whispers, and turns to go; but the young man, numb and helpless, staggers nigh to falling.

The sight of his weakness makes her strong. A mighty power thrills her body. Stooping beneath his outstretched arms grasping at the air for support, Tusee lifts him upon her broad shoulders. With half-running, triumphant steps she carries him away into the open night.

# A DREAM OF HER GRANDFATHER

HER GRANDFATHER WAS a Dakota "medicine man." Among the Indians of his day he was widely known for his successful healing work. He was one of the leading men of the tribe and came to Washington, D.C., with one of the first delegations relative to affairs concerning the Indian people and the United States government.

His was the first band of the Great Sioux Nation to make treaties with the government in the hope of bringing about an amicable arrangement between the red and white Americans. The journey to the nation's capital was made almost entirely on pony-back, there being no railroads, and the Sioux delegation was beset with many hardships on the trail. His visit to Washington, in behalf of peace among men, proved to be his last earthly mission. From a sudden illness, he died and was buried here.

When his small granddaughter grew up she learned the white man's tongue, and followed in the footsteps of her grandfather to the very seat of government to carry on his humanitarian work. Though her days were filled with problems for welfare work among her people, she had a strange dream one night during her stay in Washington. The dream was this: Returning from an afternoon out, she found a large cedar chest had been delivered to her home in her absence. She sniffed the sweet perfume of the red wood, which reminded her of the breath of the forest,—and admired the box so neatly made, without trimmings. It looked so clean, strong and durable in its native genuineness. With elation, she took the tag in her hand and read her name aloud. "Who sent me this cedar chest?" she asked, and was told it came from her grandfather.

Wondering what gift it could be her grandfather wished now to confer upon her, wholly disregarding his death years ago, she was all eagerness to open the mystery chest.

She remembered her childhood days and the stories she loved to hear about the unusual powers of her grandfather,—recalled how she, the wee girl, had coveted the medicine bags, beaded and embroidered in porcupine quills, in symbols designed by the great "medicine man," her grandfather. Well did she remember her merited rebuke that such things were never made for relics. Treasures came in due time to those ready to receive them.

In great expectancy, she lifted the heavy lid of the cedar chest. "Oh!" she exclaimed, with a note of disappointment, seeing no beaded Indian regalia or trinkets. "Why does my grandfather send such a light gift in a heavy, large box?" She was mystified and much perplexed.

The gift was a fantastic thing, of texture far more delicate than a spider's filmy web. It was a vision! A picture of an Indian camp, not painted on canvas nor yet written. It was dream-stuff, suspended in the thin air, filling the inclosure of the cedar wood container. As she looked upon it, the picture grew more and more real, exceeding the proportions of the chest. It was all so illusive a breath might have blown it away; yet there it was, real as life,—a circular camp of white cone-shaped tepees, astir with Indian people. The village crier, with flowing head-dress of eagle plumes, mounted on a prancing white pony, rode within the arena. Indian men, women and children stopped in groups and clusters, while bright painted faces peered out of tepee doors, to listen to the chieftain's crier.

At this point, she, too, heard the full melodious voice. She heard distinctly the Dakota words he proclaimed to the people. "Be glad! Rejoice! Look up, and see the new day dawning! Help is near! Hear me, every one."

She caught the glad tidings and was thrilled with new hope for her people.

# THE WIDESPREAD ENIGMA
# CONCERNING BLUE-STAR WOMAN

IT WAS SUMMER on the western plains. Fields of golden sunflowers facing eastward, greeted the rising sun. Blue-Star Woman, with windshorn braids of white hair over each ear, sat in the shade of her log hut before an open fire. Lonely but unmolested she dwelt here like the ground squirrel that took its abode nearby,—both through the easy tolerance of the land owner. The Indian woman held a skillet over the burning embers. A large round cake, with long slashes in its center, was baking and crowding the capacity of the frying pan.

In deep abstraction Blue-Star Woman prepared her morning meal. "Who am I?" had become the obsessing riddle of her life. She was no longer a young woman, being in her fifty-third year. In the eyes of the white man's law, it was required of her to give proof of her membership in the Sioux tribe. The unwritten law of heart prompted her naturally to say, "I am a being. I am Blue-Star Woman. A piece of earth is my birthright."

It was taught for reasons now forgot that an Indian should never pronounce his or her name in answer to any inquiry. It was probably a means of protection in the days of black magic. Be this as it may, Blue-Star Woman lived in times when this teaching was disregarded. It gained her nothing, however, to pronounce her name to the government official to whom she applied for her share of tribal land. His persistent question was always, "Who were your parents?"

Blue-Star Woman was left an orphan at a tender age. She did not remember them. They were long gone to the spirit-land,—and she could not understand why they should be recalled to earth on her account. It was another one of the old, old teachings of her race that the names of the dead should not be idly spoken. It had become a sacrilege to mention carelessly the name of any departed one, especially in matters of disputes over worldly possessions. The unfortunate circumstances of her early childhood, together with the lack of written records of a roving people, placed a formidable barrier between her and her heritage. The fact was events of far greater importance to the tribe than her reincarnation had passed unrecorded in books. The verbal reports of the old-time men and women of the tribe were varied,—some were actually contradictory. Blue-Star Woman was unable to find even a twig of her family tree.

She sharpened one end of a long stick and with it speared the fried bread when it was browned. Heedless of the hot bread's "Tsing!" in a high treble as it was lifted from the fire, she added it to the six others which had preceded it. It had been many a moon since she had had a meal of fried bread, for she was too poor to buy at any one time all the necessary ingredients, particularly the fat in which to fry it. During the breadmaking, the smoke-blackened coffeepot boiled over. The aroma of freshly made coffee smote her nostrils and roused her from the tantalizing memories.

The day before, friendly spirits, the unseen ones, had guided her aimless footsteps to her Indian neighbor's house. No sooner had she entered than she saw on the table some grocery bundles. "Iye-que, fortunate one!" she exclaimed as she took the straight-backed chair offered her. At once the Indian hostess untied the bundles and measured out a cupful of green coffee beans and a pound of lard. She gave them to Blue-Star Woman, saying, "I want to share my good fortune. Take these home with you." Thus it was that Blue-Star Woman had come into the unexpected possession of the materials which now contributed richly to her breakfast.

The generosity of her friend had often saved her from starvation. Generosity is said to be a fault of Indian people, but neither the Pilgrim Fathers nor Blue-Star Woman ever held it seriously against them. Blue-Star Woman was even grateful for this gift of food. She was fond of coffee,—that black drink brought hither by those daring voyagers of long ago. The coffee habit was one of the signs of her progress in the white man's civilization, also had she emerged from the tepee into a log hut, another achievement. She had learned to read the primer and to write her name. Little Blue-Star attended school unhindered by a fond mother's fears that a foreign teacher might not spare the rod with her darling.

Blue-Star Woman was her individual name. For untold ages the Indian race had not used family names. A new-born child was given a brand-new name. Blue-Star Woman was proud to write her name for which she would not be required to substitute another's upon her marriage, as is the custom of civilized peoples.

"The times are changed now," she muttered under her breath. "My individual name seems to mean nothing." Looking out into space, she saw the nodding sunflowers, and they acquiesced with her. Their drying leaves reminded her of the near approach of autumn. Then soon, very soon, the ice would freeze along the banks of the muddy river. The day of the first ice was her birthday. She would be fifty-four winters old. How futile had been all these winters to secure her a share in tribal lands. A weary smile flickered across her face as she sat there on the ground like a bronze figure of patience and long-suffering.

The breadmaking was finished. The skillet was set aside to cool. She poured the appetizing coffee into her tin cup. With fried bread and black coffee she regaled herself. Again her mind reverted to her riddle. "The missionary preacher said he could not explain the white man's law to me. He who reads daily from the Holy Bible, which he tells me is God's book, cannot understand mere man's laws. This also puzzles me," thought she to herself. "Once a wise leader of our people, addressing a president of this country, said: 'I am a man. You are another. The Great Spirit is our witness!' This is simple and easy to understand, but the times are changed. The white man's laws are strange."

Blue-Star Woman broke off a piece of fried bread between a thumb and forefinger. She ate it hungrily, and sipped from her cup of fragrant coffee. "I do not understand the white man's law. It's like walking in the dark. In this darkness, I am growing fearful of everything."

Oblivious to the world, she had not heard the footfall of two Indian men who now stood before her.

Their short-cropped hair looked blue-black in contrast to the faded civilian clothes they wore. Their white man's shoes were rusty and unpolished. To the unconventional eyes of the old Indian woman, their celluloid collars appeared like shining marks of civilization. Blue-Star Woman looked up from the lap of mother earth without rising. "Hinnu, hinnu!" she ejaculated in undisguised surprise. "Pray, who are these would-be white men?" she inquired.

In one voice and by an assumed relationship the two Indian men addressed her. "Aunt, I shake hands with you." Again Blue-Star Woman remarked, "Oh, indeed! these near white men speak my native tongue and shake hands according to our custom." Did she guess the truth, she would have known they were simply deluded mortals, deceiving others and themselves most of all. Boisterously laughing and making conversation, they each in turn gripped her withered hand.

Like a sudden flurry of wind, tossing loose ends of things, they broke into her quiet morning hour and threw her groping thoughts into greater chaos. Masking their real errand with long-drawn faces, they feigned a concern for her welfare only. "We come to ask how you are living. We heard you were slowly starving to death. We heard you are one of those Indians who have been cheated out of their share in tribal lands by the government officials."

Blue-Star Woman became intensely interested.

"You see we are educated in the white man's ways," they said with protruding chests. One unconsciously thrust his thumbs into the armholes of his ill-fitting coat and strutted about in his pride. "We can help you get your land. We want to help our aunt. All old people like you ought to be helped before the younger ones. The old will die soon, and they may never get the benefit of their land unless some one like us helps them to get their rights, without further delay."

Blue-Star Woman listened attentively.

Motioning to the mats she spread upon the ground, she said: "Be seated, my nephews." She accepted the relationship assumed for the occasion. "I will give you some breakfast." Quickly she set before them a generous helping of fried bread and cups of coffee. Resuming her own meal, she continued, "You are wonderfully kind. It is true, my nephews, that I have grown old trying to secure my share of land. It may not be long till I shall pass under the sod."

The two men responded with "How, how," which meant, "Go on with your story. We are all ears." Blue-Star Woman had not yet detected any particular sharpness about their ears, but by an impulse she looked up into their faces and scrutinized them. They were busily engaged in eating. Their eyes were fast upon the food in front of their crossed shins. Inwardly she made a passing observation how, like ravenous wolves, her nephews devoured their food. Coyotes in midwinter could not have been more starved. Without comment she offered them the remaining fried cakes, and between them they took it all. She offered the second helping of coffee, which they accepted without hesitancy. Filling their cups, she placed her empty coffeepot on the dead ashes.

To them she rehearsed her many hardships. It had become a habit now to tell her long story of disappointments with all its petty details. It was only another instance of good intentions gone awry. It was a paradox upon a land of prophecy that its path to future glory be stained with the blood of its aborigines. Incongruous as it is, the two nephews, with their white associates, were glad of a condition so profitable to them. Their solicitation for Blue-Star Woman was not at all altruistic. They thrived in their grafting business. They and their occupation were the by-product of an unwieldy bureaucracy over the nation's wards.

"Dear aunt, you failed to establish the facts of your identity," they told her. Hereupon Blue-Star Woman's countenance fell. It was ever the same old words. It was the old song of the government official she loathed to hear. The next remark restored her courage. "If any one can discover evidence, it's us! I tell you, aunt, we'll fix it all up for you." It was a great relief to the old Indian woman to be thus unburdened of her riddle, with a prospect of possessing land. "There is one thing you will have to do,—that is, to pay us one half of your land and money when you get them." Here was a pause, and Blue-Star Woman answered slowly, "Y-e-s,"in an uncertain frame of mind.

The shrewd schemers noted her behavior. "Wouldn't you rather have a half of a crust of bread than none at all?" they asked. She was duly impressed with the force of their argument. In her heart she agreed, "A little something to eat is better than nothing!" The two men talked in regular relays. The flow of smooth words was continuous and so much like purring that all the woman's suspicions were put soundly to sleep. "Look here, aunt, you know very well that prairie fire is met with a back-fire." Blue-Star Woman, recalling her experiences in fire-fighting, quickly responded, "Yes, oh, yes."

"In just the same way, we fight crooks with crooks. We have clever white lawyers working with us. They are the back-fire." Then, as if remembering some particular incident, they both laughed aloud and said, "Yes, and sometimes they use us as the back-fire! We trade fifty-fifty."

Blue-Star Woman sat with her chin in the palm of one hand with elbow resting in the other. She rocked herself slightly forward and backward. At length she answered, "Yes, I will pay you half of my share in tribal land and money when I get them. In bygone days, brave young men of the order of the White-Horse-Riders sought out the aged, the poor, the widows and orphans to aid them, but they did their good work without pay. The White-Horse-Riders are gone. The times are changed. I am a poor old Indian woman. I need warm clothing before winter begins to blow its icicles through us. I need fire wood. I need food. As you have said, a little help is better than none."

Hereupon the two pretenders scored another success.

They rose to their feet. They had eaten up all the fried bread and drained the coffeepot. They shook hands with Blue-Star Woman and departed. In the quiet that followed their departure, she sat munching her small piece of bread, which, by a lucky chance, she had taken on her plate before the hungry wolves had come. Very slowly she ate the fragment of fried bread as if to increase it by diligent mastication. A self-condemning sense of guilt disturbed her. In her dire need she had become involved with tricksters. Her nephews laughingly told her, "We use crooks, and crooks use us in the skirmish over Indian lands."

The friendly shade of the house shrank away from her and hid itself under the narrow eaves of the dirt covered roof. She shrugged her shoulders. The sun high in the sky had witnessed the affair and now glared down upon her white head. Gathering upon her arm the mats and cooking utensils, she hobbled into her log hut.

Under the brooding wilderness silence, on the Sioux Indian Reservation, the superintendent summoned together the leading Indian men of the tribe. He read a letter which he had received from headquarters in Washington, D. C. It announced the enrollment of Blue-Star Woman on their tribal roll of members and the approval of allotting land to her.

It came as a great shock to the tribesmen. Without their knowledge and consent their property was given to a strange woman. They protested in vain. The superintendent said, "I received this letter from Washington. I have read it to you for your information. I have fulfilled my duty. I can do no more." With these fateful words he dismissed the assembly.

Heavy hearted, Chief High Flier returned to his dwelling. Smoking his long-stemmed pipe he pondered over the case of Blue-Star Woman. The Indian's guardian had got into a way of usurping autocratic power in disposing of the wards' property. It was growing intolerable. "No doubt this Indian woman is entitled to allotment, but where? Certainly not here," he thought to himself.

Laying down his pipe, he called his little granddaughter from her play. "You are my interpreter and scribe," he said. "Bring your paper and pencil." A letter was written in the child's sprawling hand, and signed by the old chieftain. It read:

"My Friend:
"I make letter to you. My heart is sad. Washington give my tribe's land to a woman called Blue-Star. We do not know her. We were not asked to give land, but our land is taken from us to give to another Indian. This is not right. Lots of little children of my tribe have no land. Why this strange woman get our land which belongs to our children? Go to Washington and ask if our treaties tell him to give our property away without asking us. Tell him I thought we made good treaties on paper, but now our children cry for food. We are too poor. We cannot give even to our own little children. Washington is very rich. Washington now owns our country. If he wants to help this poor Indian woman, Blue-Star, let him give her some of his land and his money. This is all I will say until you answer me. I shake hands with you with my heart. The Great Spirit hears my words. They are true.

"Your friend,
"Chief High Flier.
"X (his mark.)"

The letter was addressed to a prominent American woman. A stamp was carefully placed on the envelope.

Early the next morning, before the dew was off the grass, the chieftain's riding pony was caught from the pasture and brought to his log house. It was saddled and bridled by a younger man, his son with whom he made his home. The old chieftain came out, carrying in one hand his long-stemmed pipe and tobacco pouch. His blanket was loosely girdled about his waist. Tightly holding the saddle horn, he placed a moccasined foot carefully into the stirrup and pulled himself awkwardly into the saddle, muttering to himself, "Alas, I can no more leap into my saddle. I now must crawl about in my helplessness." He was past eighty years of age, and no longer agile.

He set upon his ten-mile trip to the only post office for hundreds of miles around. In his shirt pocket, he carried the letter destined, in due season, to reach the heart of American people. His pony, grown old in service, jogged along the dusty road. Memories of other days thronged the wayside, and for the lonely rider transformed all the country. Those days were gone when the Indian youths were taught to be truthful,—to be merciful to the poor. Those days were gone when moral cleanliness was a chief virtue; when public feasts were given in honor of the virtuous girls and young men of the tribe. Untold mischief is now possible through these broken ancient laws. The younger generation were not being properly trained in the high virtues. A slowly starving race was growing mad, and the pitifully weak sold their lands for a pot of porridge.

"He, he, he! He, he, he!" he lamented. "Small Voice Woman, my own relative is being represented as the mother of this strange Blue-Star—the papers were made by two young Indian men who have learned the white man's ways. Why must I be forced to accept the mischief of children? My memory is clear. My reputation for veracity is well known.

Small Voice Woman lived in my house until her death. She had only one child and it was a *boy!* He held his hand over this thumping heart, and was reminded of the letter in his pocket. "This letter,—what will happen when it reaches my good friend?" he asked himself. The chieftain rubbed his dim eyes and groaned, "If only my good friend knew the folly of turning my letter into the hands of bureaucrats! In face of repeated defeat, I am daring once more to send this one letter." An inner voice said in his ear, "And this one letter will share the same fate of the other letters."

Startled by the unexpected voice, he jerked upon the bridle reins and brought the drowsy pony to a sudden halt. There was no one near. He found himself a mile from the post office, for the cluster of government buildings, where lived the superintendent, were now in plain sight. His thin frame shook with emotion. He could not go there with his letter.

He dismounted from his pony. His quavering voice chanted a bravery song as he gathered dry grasses and the dead stalks of last year's sunflowers. He built a fire, and crying aloud, for his sorrow was greater than he could bear, he cast the letter into the flames. The fire consumed it. He sent his message on the wings of fire and he believed she would get it. He yet trusted that help would come to his people before it was too late. The pony tossed his head in readiness to go. He knew he was on the return trip and he was glad to travel.

The wind which blew so gently at dawn was now increased into a gale as the sun approached the zenith. The chieftain, on his way home, sensed a coming storm. He looked upward to the sky and around in every direction. Behind him, in the distance, he saw a cloud of dust. He saw several horsemen whipping their ponies and riding at great speed. Occasionally he heard their shouts, as if calling after some one. He slackened his pony's pace and frequently looked over his shoulder to see who the riders were advancing in hot haste upon him. He was growing curious. In a short time the riders surrounded him. On their coats shone brass buttons, and on their hats were gold cords and tassels. They were Indian police.

"Wan!" he exclaimed, finding himself the object of their chase. It was their foolish ilk who had murdered the great leader, Sitting Bull. "Pray, what is the joke? Why do young men surround an old man quietly riding home?"

"Uncle," said the spokesman, "we are hirelings, as you know. We are sent by the government superintendent to arrest you and take you back with us. The superintendent says you are one of the bad Indians, singing war songs and opposing the government all the time; this morning you were seen trying to set fire to the government agency."

"Hunhunhe!" replied the old chief, placing the palm of his hand over his mouth agape in astonishment. "All this is unbelievable!"

The policeman took hold of the pony's bridle and turned the reluctant little beast around. They led it back with them and the old chieftain sat unresisting in the saddle. High Flier was taken before the superintendent, who charged him with setting fires to destroy government buildings and found him guilty. Thus Chief High Flier was sent to jail. He had already suffered much during his life. He was the voiceless man of America. And now in his old age he was cast into prison. The chagrin of it all, together with his utter helplessness to defend his own or his people's human rights, weighed heavily upon his spirit.

The foul air of the dingy cell nauseated him who loved the open. He sat wearily down upon the tattered mattress, which lay on the rough board floor. He drew his robe closely about his tall figure, holding it partially over his face, his hands covered within the folds. In profound gloom the gray-haired prisoner sat there, without a stir for long hours and knew not when the day ended and the night began. He sat buried in his desperation. His eyes were closed, but he could not sleep. Bread and water in tin receptacles set upon the floor beside him untouched. He was not hungry. Venturesome mice crept out upon the floor and scampered in the dim starlight streaming through the iron bars of the cell window. They squeaked as they dared each other to run across his moccasined feet, but the chieftain neither saw nor heard them.

A terrific struggle was waged within his being. He fought as he never fought before. Tenaciously he hung upon hope for the day of salvation—that hope hoary with age. Defying all odds against him, he refused to surrender faith in good people.

Underneath his blanket, wrapped so closely about him, stole a luminous light. Before his stricken conscience appeared a vision. Lo, his good friend, the American woman to whom he had sent his messages by fire, now stood there a legion! A vast multitude of women, with uplifted hands, gazed upon a huge stone image. Their upturned faces were eager and very earnest. The stone figure was that of a woman upon the brink of the Great Waters, facing eastward. The myriad living hands remained uplifted till the stone woman began to show signs of life. Very majestically she turned around, and, lo, she smiled upon this great galaxy of American women. She was the Statue of Liberty! It was she, who, though representing human liberty, formerly turned her back upon the American aborigine. Her face was aglow with compassion. Her eyes swept across the outspread continent of America, the home of the red man.

At this moment her torch flamed brighter and whiter till its radiance reached into the obscure and remote places of the land. Her light of liberty penetrated Indian reservations. A loud shout of joy rose up from the Indians of the earth, everywhere!

All too soon the picture was gone. Chief High Flier awoke. He lay prostrate on the floor where during the night he had fallen. He rose and took his seat again upon the mattress. Another day was ushered into his life. In his heart lay the secret vision of hope born in the midnight of his sorrows. It enabled him to serve his jail sentence with a mute dignity which baffled those who saw him.

Finally came the day of his release. There was rejoicing over all the land. The desolate hills that harbored wailing voices nightly now were hushed and still. Only gladness filled the air. A crowd gathered round the jail to greet the chieftain. His son stood at the entrance way, while the guard unlocked the prison door. Serenely quiet, the old Indian chief stepped forth. An unseen stone in his path caused him to stumble slightly, but his son grasped him by the hand and steadied his tottering steps. He led him to a heavy lumber wagon drawn by a small pony team which he had brought to take him home. The people thronged about him—hundreds shook hands with him and went away singing native songs of joy for the safe return to them of their absent one.

Among the happy people came Blue-Star Woman's two nephews. Each shook the chieftain's hand. One of them held out an ink pad saying, "We are glad we were able to get you out of jail. We have great influence with the Indian Bureau in Washington, D. C. When you need help, let us know. Here press your thumb in this pad." His companion took from his pocket a document prepared for the old chief's signature, and held it on the wagon wheel for the thumb mark. The chieftain was taken by surprise. He looked into his son's eyes to know the meaning of these two men. "It is our agreement," he explained to his old father. "I pledged to pay them half of your land if they got you out of jail."

The old chieftain sighed, but made no comment. Words were vain. He pressed his indelible thumb mark, his signature it was, upon the deed, and drove home with his son.

# AMERICA'S
# INDIAN PROBLEM

THE HOSPITALITY OF the American aborigine, it is told, saved the early settlers from starvation during the first bleak winters. In commemoration of having been so well received, Newport erected "a cross as a sign of English dominion." With sweet words he quieted the suspicions of Chief Powhatan, his friend. He "told him that the arms (of the cross) represented Powhatan and himself, and the middle their united league."

DeSoto and his Spaniards were graciously received by the Indian Princess Cofachiqui in the South. While on a sight-seeing tour they entered the ancestral tombs of those Indians. DeSoto "dipped into the pearls and gave his two joined hands full to each cavalier to make rosaries of, he said, to say prayers for their sins on. We imagine if their prayers were in proportion to their sins they must have spent the most of their time at their devotions."

It was in this fashion that the old world snatched away the fee in the land of the new. It was in this fashion that America was divided between the powers of Europe and the aborigines were dispossessed of their country. The barbaric rule of might from which the paleface had fled hither for refuge caught up with him again, and in the melee the hospitable native suffered "legal disability."

History tells that it was from the English and the Spanish our government inherited its legal victims, the American Indians, whom to this day we hold as wards and not as citizens of their own freedom loving land. A long century of dishonor followed this inheritance of somebody's loot. Now the time is at hand when the American Indian shall have his day in court through the help of the women of America. The stain upon America's fair name is to be removed, and the remnant of the Indian nation, suffering from malnutrition, is to number among the invited invisible guests at your dinner tables.

In this undertaking there must be cooperation of head, heart and hand. We serve both our own government and a voiceless people within our midst. We would open the door of American opportunity to the red man and encourage him to find his rightful place in our American life. We would remove the barriers that hinder his normal development.

Wardship is no substitute for American citizenship, therefore we seek his enfranchisement. The many treaties made in good faith with the Indian by our government we would like to see equitably settled. By a constructive program we hope to do away with the "piecemeal legislation" affecting Indians here and there which has proven an exceedingly expensive and disappointing method.

Do you know what *your* Bureau of Indian Affairs, in Washington, D. C., really is? How it is organized and how it deals with wards of the nation? This is our first study. Let us be informed of facts and then we may formulate our opinions. In the remaining space allowed me I shall quote from the report of the Bureau of Municipal Research, in their investigation of the Indian Bureau, published by them in the September issue, 1915, No. 65, "Municipal Research," 261 Broadway, New York City. This report is just as good for our use today as when it was first made, for very little, if any, change has been made in the administration of Indian Affairs since then.

### Prefatory Note

"While this report was printed for the information of the members of Congress, it was not made a part of the report of the Joint Commission of Congress, at whose request it was prepared, and is not available for distribution."

### Unpublished Digest of Statutory and Treaty Provisions Governing Indian Funds

"When in 1913 inquiry was made into the accounting and reporting methods of the Indian Office by the President's Commission on Economy and Efficiency, it was found there was no digest of the provisions of statutes and treaties with Indian tribes governing

Indian funds and trust obligations of the government. Such a digest was therefore prepared. It was not completed, however, until after Congress adjourned March 4, 1913. Then, instead of being published, it found its way into the pigeon-holes in the Interior Department and the Civil Service Commission, where the working papers and unpublished reports of the commission were ordered stored. The digest itself would make a document of about three hundred pages.

## Unpublished Outline of Organization

"By order of the President, the commission, in cooperation with various persons assigned to this work, also prepared at great pains a complete analysis of the organization of every department, office and commission of the federal government as of July 1, 1912. This represented a complete picture of the government as a whole in summary outline; it also represented an accurate picture of every administrative bureau, office, and of every operative or field station, and showed in his working relation each of the 500,000 officers and employees in the public service. The report in typewritten form was one of the working documents used in the preparation of the 'budget' submitted by President Taft to Congress in February, 1913. The 'budget' was ordered printed by Congress, but the cost thereof was to be charged against the President's appropriation. There was not enough money remaining in this appropriation to warrant the printing of the report on organization. It, therefore, also found repose in a dark closet."

## Too Voluminous to Be Made Part of This Series

"Congress alone could make the necessary provision for the publication of these materials; the documents are too voluminous to be printed as a part of this series, even if official permission were granted. It is again suggested, however, that the data might be made readily accessible and available to students by placing in the manuscript division of the Library of Congress one copy of the unpublished reports and working papers of the President's Commission on Economy and Efficiency. This action was recommended by the commission, but the only official action taken was to order that the materials be placed under lock and key in the Civil Service Commission."

## Need for Special Care in Management

"The need for special care in the management of Indian Affairs lies in the fact that in theory of law the Indian has not the rights of a citizen. He has not even the rights of a foreign resident. The Indian individually does not have access to the courts; he can not individually appeal to the administrative and judicial branches of the public service for the enforcement of his rights. He himself is considered as a ward of the United States. His property and funds are held in trust. ★ ★ ★ The Indian Office is the agency of the government for administering both the guardianship of the Indian and the trusteeship of his properties."

## Conditions Adverse to Good Administration

"The legal status of the Indian and his property is the condition which makes it incumbent on the government to assume the obligation of protector. What is of special interest in this inquiry is to note the conditions under which the Indian Office has been required to conduct its business. In no other relation are the agents of the government under conditions more adverse to efficient administration. The influence which make for the infidelity to trusteeship, for subversion of properties and funds, for the violation of physical and moral welfare have been powerful. The opportunities and inducements are much greater than those which have operated with ruinous effect on other branches of public service and on the trustees and officers of our great private corporations. In many instances, the integrity of these have been broken down."

## Government Machinery Inadequate

"★ ★ ★ Behind the sham protection, which operated largely as a blind to publicity, have been at all times great wealth in the form of Indian funds to be subverted; valuable lands, mines, oil fields, and other natural resources to be despoiled or appropriated to the use of the trader; and large profits to be made by those dealing with trustees who were animated by motives of gain. This has been the situation in which the Indian Service has been for more than a century—the Indian during all this time having his rights and properties to greater or less extent neglected; the guardian, the government, in many instances, passive to conditions which have contributed to his undoing."

## Opportunities Still Present

"And still, due to the increasing value of his remaining estate, there is left an inducement to fraud, corruption, and institutional incompetence almost beyond the possibility of comprehension. The properties and funds of the Indians today are estimated at not less than one thousand millions of dollars. There is still a great obligation to be discharged, which must run through many years. The government itself owes many millions of dollars for Indian moneys which it has converted to its own use, and it is of interest to note that it does not know and the officers do not know what is the present condition of the Indian funds in their keeping."

## Primary Defects

"★ ★ ★ The story of the mismanagement of Indian Affairs is only a chapter in the history of the mismanagement of corporate trusts. The Indian has been the victim of the same kind of neglect, the same abortive processes, the same malpractices as have the life insurance policyholders, the bank depositor, the industrial and transportation shareholder. The form of organization of the trusteeship has been one which does not provide for independent audit and supervision. The institutional methods and practices have been such that they do not provide either a fact basis for official judgment or publicity of facts which, if made available, would supply evidence of infidelity. In the operation of this machinery, there has not been the means provided for effective official scrutiny and the public conscience could not be reached."

## Ample Precedents to Be Followed

"Precedents to be followed are ample. In private corporate trusts that have been mismanaged a basis of appeal has been found only when some favorable circumstance has brought to light conditions so shocking as to cause those people who have possessed political power, as a matter of self-protection, to demand a thorough reorganization and revision of methods. The same motive has lain back of legislation for the Indian. But the motive to political action has been less effective, for the reason that in the past the Indians who have acted in self-protection have either been killed or placed in confinement. All the machinery of government has been set to work to repress rather than to provide adequate means for justly dealing with a large population which had no political rights."

—Edict Magazine.

# Old Indian Legends

# PREFACE

THESE LEGENDS ARE relics of our country's once virgin soil. These and many others are the tales the little black-haired aborigine loved so much to hear beside the night fire.

For him the personified elements and other spirits played in a vast world right around the center fire of the wigwam.

Iktomi, the snare weaver, Iya, the Eater, and Old Double-Face are not wholly fanciful creatures.

There were other worlds of legendary folk for the young aborigine, such as "The Star-Men of the Sky," "The Thunder Birds Blinking Zigzag Lightning," and "The Mysterious Spirits of Trees and Flowers."

Under an open sky, nestling close to the earth, the old Dakota story-tellers have told me these legends. In both Dakotas, North and South, I have often listened to the same story told over again by a new story-teller.

While I recognized such a legend without the least difficulty, I found the renderings varying much in little incidents. Generally one helped the other in restoring some lost link in the original character of the tale. And now I have tried to transplant the native spirit of these tales—root and all—into the English language, since America in the last few centuries has acquired a second tongue.

The old legends of America belong quite as much to the blue-eyed little patriot as to the black-haired aborigine. And when they are grown tall like the wise grown-ups may they not lack interest in a further study of Indian folklore, a study which so strongly suggests our near kinship with the rest of humanity and points a steady finger toward the great brotherhood of mankind, and by which one is so forcibly impressed with the possible earnestness of life as seen through the teepee door! If it be true that much lies "in the eye of the beholder," then in the American aborigine as in any other race, sincerity of belief, though it were based upon mere optical illusion, demands a little respect.

After all he seems at heart much like other peoples.

ZITKALA-ŠA

# IKTOMI AND THE DUCKS

IKTOMI IS A spider fairy. He wears brown deerskin leggins with long soft fringes on either side, and tiny beaded moccasins on his feet. His long black hair is parted in the middle and wrapped with red, red bands. Each round braid hangs over a small brown ear and falls forward over his shoulders.

He even paints his funny face with red and yellow, and draws big black rings around his eyes. He wears a deerskin jacket, with bright colored beads sewed tightly on it. Iktomi dresses like a real Dakota brave. In truth, his paint and deerskins are the best part of him—if ever dress is part of man or fairy.

Iktomi is a wily fellow. His hands are always kept in mischief. He prefers to spread a snare rather than to earn the smallest thing with honest hunting. Why! he laughs outright with wide open mouth when some simple folk are caught in a trap, sure and fast.

He never dreams another lives so bright as he. Often his own conceit leads him hard against the common sense of simpler people.

Poor Iktomi cannot help being a little imp. And so long as he is a naughty fairy, he cannot find a single friend. No one helps him when he is in trouble. No one really loves him. Those who come to admire his handsome beaded jacket and long fringed leggins soon go away sick and tired of his vain, vain words and heartless laughter.

Thus Iktomi lives alone in a cone-shaped wigwam upon the plain. One day he sat hungry within his teepee. Suddenly he rushed out, dragging after him his blanket. Quickly spreading it on the ground, he tore up dry tall grass with both his hands and tossed it fast into the blanket.

Tying all the four corners together in a knot, he threw the light bundle of grass over his shoulder.

Snatching up a slender willow stick with his free left hand, he started off with a hop and a leap. From side to side bounced the bundle on his back, as he ran light-footed over the uneven ground. Soon he came to the edge of the great level land. On the hilltop he paused for breath. With wicked smacks of his dry parched lips, as if tasting some tender meat, he looked straight into space toward the marshy river bottom. With a thin palm shading his eyes from the western sun, he peered far away into the lowlands, munching his own cheeks all the while. "Ah-ha!" grunted he, satisfied with what he saw.

A group of wild ducks were dancing and feasting in the marshes. With wings outspread, tip to tip, they moved up and down in a large circle. Within the ring, around a small drum, sat the chosen singers, nodding their heads and blinking their eyes.

They sang in unison a merry dance-song, and beat a lively tattoo on the drum.

Following a winding footpath near by, came a bent figure of a Dakota brave. He bore on his back a very large bundle. With a willow cane he propped himself up as he staggered along beneath his burden.

"Ho! who is there?" called out a curious old duck, still bobbing up and down in the circular dance.

Hereupon the drummers stretched their necks till they strangled their song for a look at the stranger passing by.

"Ho, Iktomi! Old fellow, pray tell us what you carry in your blanket. Do not hurry off! Stop! halt!" urged one of the singers.

"Stop! stay! Show us what is in your blanket!" cried out other voices.

"My friends, I must not spoil your dance. Oh, you would not care to see if you only knew what is in my blanket. Sing on! dance on! I must not show you what I carry on my back," answered Iktomi, nudging his own sides with his elbows. This reply broke up the ring entirely. Now all the ducks crowded about Iktomi.

"We must see what you carry! We must know what is in your blanket!" they shouted in both his ears. Some even brushed their wings against the mysterious bundle. Nudging himself again, wily Iktomi said, "My friends, 'tis only a pack of songs I carry in my blanket."

"Oh, then let us hear your songs!" cried the curious ducks.

At length Iktomi consented to sing his songs. With delight all the ducks flapped their wings and cried together, "Hoye! hoye!"

Iktomi, with great care, laid down his bundle on the ground.

"I will build first a round straw house, for I never sing my songs in the open air," said he.

Quickly he bent green willow sticks, planting both ends of each pole into the earth. These he covered thick with reeds and grasses. Soon the straw hut was ready. One by one the fat ducks waddled in through a small opening, which was the only entrance way. Beside the door Iktomi stood smiling, as the ducks, eyeing his bundle of songs, strutted into the hut.

In a strange low voice Iktomi began his queer old tunes. All the ducks sat round-eyed in a circle about the mysterious singer. It was dim in that straw hut, for Iktomi had not forgot to cover up the small entrance way. All of a sudden his song burst into full voice. As the startled ducks sat uneasily on the ground, Iktomi changed his tune into a minor strain. These were the words he sang:

"Istokmus wacipo, tuwayatunwanpi kinhan išta nišašapi kta," which is, "With eyes closed you must dance. He who dares to open his eyes, forever red eyes shall have."

Up rose the circle of seated ducks and holding their wings close against their sides began to dance to the rhythm of Iktomi's song and drum.

With eyes closed they did dance! Iktomi ceased to beat his drum. He began to sing louder and faster. He seemed to be moving about in the center of the ring. No duck dared blink a wink. Each one shut his eyes very tight and danced even harder. Up and down! Shifting to the right of them they hopped round and round in that blind dance. It was a difficult dance for the curious folk.

At length one of the dancers could close his eyes no longer! It was a Skiska who peeped the least tiny blink at Iktomi within the center of the circle. "Oh! oh!" squawked he in awful terror! "Run! fly! Iktomi is twisting your heads and breaking your necks! Run out and fly! fly!" he cried. Hereupon the ducks opened their eyes. There beside Iktomi's bundle of songs lay half of their crowd—flat on their backs.

Out they flew through the opening Skiska had made as he rushed forth with his alarm.

But as they soared high into the blue sky they cried to one another: "Oh! your eyes are red-red!" "And yours are red-red!" For the warning words of the magic minor strain had proven true. "Ah-ha!" laughed Iktomi, untying the four corners of his blanket, "I shall sit no more hungry within my dwelling." Homeward he trudged along with nice fat ducks in his blanket. He left the little straw hut for the rains and winds to pull down.

Having reached his own teepee on the high level lands, Iktomi kindled a large fire out of doors. He planted sharp-pointed sticks around the leaping flames. On each stake he fastened a duck to roast. A few he buried under the ashes to bake. Disappearing within his teepee, he came out again with some huge seashells. These were his dishes. Placing one under each roasting duck, he muttered, "The sweet fat oozing out will taste well with the hard-cooked breasts."

Heaping more willows upon the fire, Iktomi sat down on the ground with crossed shins. A long chin between his knees pointed toward the red flames, while his eyes were on the browning ducks.

Just above his ankles he clasped and unclasped his long bony fingers. Now and then he sniffed impatiently the savory odor.

The brisk wind which stirred the fire also played with a squeaky old tree beside Iktomi's wigwam.

From side to side the tree was swaying and crying in an old man's voice, "Help! I'll break! I'll fall!" Iktomi shrugged his great shoulders, but did not once take his eyes from the ducks. The dripping of amber oil into pearly dishes, drop by drop, pleased his hungry eyes. Still the old tree man called for help. "Hĕ! What sound is it that makes my ear ache!" exclaimed Iktomi, holding a hand on his ear.

He rose and looked around. The squeaking came from the tree. Then he began climbing the tree to find the disagreeable sound. He placed his foot right on a cracked limb without seeing it. Just then a whiff of wind came rushing by and pressed together the broken edges. There in a strong wooden hand Iktomi's foot was caught.

"Oh! my foot is crushed!" he howled like a coward. In vain he pulled and puffed to free himself.

While sitting a prisoner on the tree he spied, through his tears, a pack of gray wolves roaming over the level lands. Waving his hands toward them, he called in his loudest voice, "He! Gray wolves! Don't you come here! I'm caught fast in the tree so that my duck feast is getting cold. Don't you come to eat up my meal."

The leader of the pack upon hearing Iktomi's words turned to his comrades and said:

"Ah! hear the foolish fellow! He says he has a duck feast to be eaten! Let us hurry there for our share!" Away bounded the wolves toward Iktomi's lodge.

From the tree Iktomi watched the hungry wolves eat up his nicely browned fat ducks. His foot pained him more and more. He heard them crack the small round bones with their strong long teeth and eat out the oily marrow. Now severe pains shot up from his foot through his whole body. "Hin-hin-hin!" sobbed Iktomi. Real tears washed brown streaks across his red-painted cheeks. Smacking their lips, the wolves began to leave the place, when Iktomi cried out like a pouting child, "At least you have left my baking under the ashes!"

"Ho! po!" shouted the mischievous wolves; "he says more ducks are to be found under the ashes! Come! Let us have our fill this once!"

Running back to the dead fire, they pawed out the ducks with such rude haste that a cloud of ashes rose like gray smoke over them.

"Hin-hin-hin!" moaned Iktomi, when the wolves had scampered off. All too late, the sturdy breeze returned, and, passing by, pulled apart the broken edges of the tree. Iktomi was released. But alas! he had no duck feast.

# IKTOMI'S BLANKET

ALONE WITHIN HIS teepee sat Iktomi. The sun was but a hand's-breadth from the western edge of land.

"Those bad, bad gray wolves! They ate up all my nice fat ducks!" muttered he, rocking his body to and fro.

He was cuddling the evil memory he bore those hungry wolves. At last he ceased to sway his body backward and forward, but sat still and stiff as a stone image.

"Oh! I'll go to Inyan, the great-grandfather, and pray for food!" he exclaimed.

At once he hurried forth from his teepee and, with his blanket over one shoulder, drew nigh to a huge rock on a hillside.

With half-crouching, half-running strides, he fell upon Inyan with outspread hands.

"Grandfather! pity me. I am hungry. I am starving. Give me food. Great-grandfather, give me meat to eat!" he cried. All the while he stroked and caressed the face of the great stone god.

The all-powerful Great Spirit, who makes the trees and grass, can hear the voice of those who pray in many varied ways. The hearing of Inyan, the large hard stone, was the one most sought after. He was the great-grandfather, for he had sat upon the hillside many, many seasons. He had seen the prairie put on a snow-white blanket and then change it for a bright green robe more than a thousand times.

Still unaffected by the myriad moons, he rested on the everlasting hill, listening to the prayers of Indian warriors. Before the finding of the magic arrow he had sat there.

Now, as Iktomi prayed and wept before the great-grandfather, the sky in the west was red like a glowing face. The sunset poured a soft mellow light upon the huge gray stone and the solitary figure beside it. It was the smile of the Great Spirit upon the grandfather and the wayward child.

The prayer was heard. Iktomi knew it. "Now, grandfather, accept my offering; 'tis all I have," said Iktomi as he spread his half-worn blanket upon Inyan's cold shoulders. Then Iktomi, happy with the smile of the sunset sky, followed a footpath leading toward a thicketed ravine. He had not gone many paces into the shrubbery when before him lay a freshly wounded deer!

"This is the answer from the red western sky!" cried Iktomi with hands uplifted.

Slipping a long thin blade from out his belt, he cut large chunks of choice meat. Sharpening some willow sticks, he planted them around a wood-pile he had ready to kindle. On these stakes he meant to roast the venison.

While he was rubbing briskly two long sticks to start a fire, the sun in the west fell out of the sky below the edge of land. Twilight was over all. Iktomi felt the cold night air upon his bare neck and shoulders. "Ough!" he shivered as he wiped his knife on the grass. Tucking it in a beaded case hanging from his belt, Iktomi stood erect, looking about. He shivered again. "Ough! Ah! I am cold. I wish I had my blanket!" whispered he, hovering over the pile of dry sticks and the sharp stakes round about it. Suddenly he paused and dropped his hands at his sides.

"The old great-grandfather does not feel the cold as I do. He does not need my old blanket as I do. I wish I had not given it to him. Oh! I think I'll run up there and take it back!" said he, pointing his long chin toward the large gray stone.

Iktomi, in the warm sunshine, had no need of his blanket, and it had been very easy to part with a thing which he could not miss. But the chilly night wind quite froze his ardent thank-offering.

Thus running up the hillside, his teeth chattering all the way, he drew near to Inyan, the sacred symbol. Seizing one corner of the half-worn blanket, Iktomi pulled it off with a jerk.

"Give my blanket back, old grandfather! You do not need it. I do!" This was very wrong, yet Iktomi did it, for his wit was not wisdom. Drawing the blanket tight over his shoulders, he descended the hill with hurrying feet.

He was soon upon the edge of the ravine. A young moon, like a bright bent bow, climbed up from the southwest horizon a little way into the sky.

In this pale light Iktomi stood motionless as a ghost amid the thicket. His woodpile was not yet kindled. His pointed stakes were still bare as he had left them. But where was the deer—the venison he had felt warm in his hands a moment ago? It was gone. Only the dry rib bones lay on the ground like giant fingers from an open grave. Iktomi was troubled. At length, stooping over the white dried bones, he took hold of one and shook it. The bones, loose in their sockets, rattled together at his touch. Iktomi let go his hold. He sprang back amazed. And though he wore a blanket his teeth chattered more than ever. Then his blunted sense will surprise you, little reader; for instead of being grieved that he had taken back his blanket, he cried aloud, "Hin-hin-hin! If only I had eaten the venison before going for my blanket!"

Those tears no longer moved the hand of the Generous Giver. They were selfish tears. The Great Spirit does not heed them ever.

# IKTOMI AND THE MUSKRAT

BESIDE A WHITE lake, beneath a large grown willow tree, sat Iktomi on the bare ground. The heap of smouldering ashes told of a recent open fire. With ankles crossed together around a pot of soup, Iktomi bent over some delicious boiled fish.

Fast he dipped his black horn spoon into the soup, for he was ravenous. Iktomi had no regular meal times. Often when he was hungry he went without food.

Well hid between the lake and the wild rice, he looked nowhere save into the pot of fish. Not knowing when the next meal would be, he meant to eat enough now to last some time.

"How, how, my friend!" said a voice out of the wild rice. Iktomi started. He almost choked with his soup. He peered through the long reeds from where he sat with his long horn spoon in mid-air.

"How, my friend!" said the voice again, this time close at his side. Iktomi turned and there stood a dripping muskrat who had just come out of the lake.

"Oh, it is my friend who startled me. I wondered if among the wild rice some spirit voice was talking. How, how, my friend!" said Iktomi. The muskrat stood smiling. On his lips hung a ready "Yes, my friend," when Iktomi would ask, "My friend, will you sit down beside me and share my food?"

That was the custom of the plains people. Yet Iktomi sat silent. He hummed an old dance-song and beat gently on the edge of the pot with his buffalo-horn spoon. The muskrat began to feel awkward before such lack of hospitality and wished himself under water.

After many heart throbs Iktomi stopped drumming with his horn ladle, and looking upward into the muskrat's face, he said:

"My friend, let us run a race to see who shall win this pot of fish. If I win, I shall not need to share it with you. If you win, you shall have half of it." Springing to his feet, Iktomi began at once to tighten the belt about his waist.

"My friend Ikto, I cannot run a race with you! I am not a swift runner, and you are nimble as a deer. We shall not run any race together," answered the hungry muskrat.

For a moment Iktomi stood with a hand on his long protruding chin. His eyes were fixed upon something in the air. The muskrat looked out of the corners of his eyes without moving his head. He watched the wily Iktomi concocting a plot.

"Yes, yes," said Iktomi, suddenly turning his gaze upon the unwelcome visitor; "I shall carry a large stone on my back. That will slacken my usual speed; and the race will be a fair one."

"I shall carry a large stone on my back. That will slacken my usual speed; and the race will be a fair one."

Saying this he laid a firm hand upon the muskrat's shoulder and started off along the edge of the lake. When they reached the opposite side Iktomi pried about in search of a heavy stone.

He found one half-buried in the shallow water. Pulling it out upon dry land, he wrapped it in his blanket.

"Now, my friend, you shall run on the left side of the lake, I on the other. The race is for the boiled fish in yonder kettle!" said Iktomi.

The muskrat helped to lift the heavy stone upon Iktomi's back. Then they parted. Each took a narrow path through the tall reeds fringing the shore. Iktomi found his load a heavy one. Perspiration hung like beads on his brow. His chest heaved hard and fast.

He looked across the lake to see how far the muskrat had gone, but nowhere did he see any sign of him. "Well, he is running low under the wild rice!" said he. Yet as he scanned the tall grasses on the lake shore, he saw not one stir as if to make way for the runner. "Ah, has he gone so fast ahead that the disturbed grasses in his trail have quieted again?" exclaimed Iktomi. With that thought he quickly dropped the heavy stone. "No more of this!" said he, patting his chest with both hands.

Off with a springing bound, he ran swiftly toward the goal. Tufts of reeds and grass fell flat under his feet. Hardly had they raised their heads when Iktomi was many paces gone.

Soon he reached the heap of cold ashes. Iktomi halted stiff as if he had struck an invisible cliff. His black eyes showed a ring of white about them as he stared at the empty ground. There was no pot of boiled fish! There was no water-man in sight! "Oh, if only I had shared my food like a real Dakota, I would not have lost it all! Why did I not know the muskrat would run through the water? He swims faster than I could ever run! That is what he has done. He has laughed at me for carrying a weight on my back while he shot hither like an arrow!"

Crying thus to himself, Iktomi stepped to the water's brink. He stooped forward with a hand on each bent knee and peeped far into the deep water.

"There!" he exclaimed, "I see you, my friend, sitting with your ankles wound around my little pot of fish! My friend, I am hungry. Give me a bone!"

"Ha! ha! ha!" laughed the water-man, the muskrat. The sound did not rise up out of the lake, for it came down from overhead. With his hands still on his knees, Iktomi turned his face upward into the great willow tree. Opening wide his mouth he begged, "My friend, my friend, give me a bone to gnaw!"

"Ha! ha!" laughed the muskrat, and leaning over the limb he sat upon, he let fall a small sharp bone which dropped right into Iktomi's throat. Iktomi almost choked to death before he could get it out. In the tree the muskrat sat laughing loud. "Next time, say to a visiting friend, 'Be seated beside me, my friend. Let me share with you my food.'"

# IKTOMI AND THE COYOTE

AFAR OFF UPON a large level land, a summer sun was shining bright. Here and there over the rolling green were tall bunches of coarse gray weeds. Iktomi in his fringed buckskins walked alone across the prairie with a black bare head glossy in the sunlight. He walked through the grass without following any well-worn footpath.

From one large bunch of coarse weeds to another he wound his way about the great plain. He lifted his foot lightly and placed it gently forward like a wildcat prowling noiselessly through the thick grass. He stopped a few steps away from a very large bunch of wild sage. From shoulder to shoulder he tilted his head. Still farther he bent from side to side, first low over one hip and then over the other. Far forward he stooped, stretching his long thin neck like a duck, to see what lay under a fur coat beyond the bunch of coarse grass.

A sleek gray-faced prairie wolf! his pointed black nose tucked in between his four feet drawn snugly together; his handsome bushy tail wound over his nose and feet; a coyote fast asleep in the shadow of a bunch of grass!—this is what Iktomi spied. Carefully he raised one foot and cautiously reached out with his toes. Gently, gently he lifted the foot behind and placed it before the other. Thus he came nearer and nearer to the round fur ball lying motionless under the sage grass.

Now Iktomi stood beside it, looking at the closed eyelids that did not quiver the least bit. Pressing his lips into straight lines and nodding his head slowly, he bent over the wolf. He held his ear close to the coyote's nose, but not a breath of air stirred from it.

"Dead!" said he at last. "Dead, but not long since he ran over these plains! See! there in his paw is caught a fresh feather. He is nice fat meat!" Taking hold of the paw with the bird feather fast

102

on it, he exclaimed, "Why, he is still warm! I'll carry him to my dwelling and have a roast for my evening meal. Ah-ha!" he laughed, as he seized the coyote by its two fore paws and its two hind feet and swung him over head across his shoulders. The wolf was large and the teepee was far across the prairie. Iktomi trudged along with his burden, smacking his hungry lips together. He blinked his eyes hard to keep out the salty perspiration streaming down his face.

All the while the coyote on his back lay gazing into the sky with wide open eyes. His long white teeth fairly gleamed as he smiled and smiled.

"To ride on one's own feet is tiresome, but to be carried like a warrior from a brave fight is great fun!" said the coyote in his heart. He had never been borne on any one's back before and the new experience delighted him. He lay there lazily on Iktomi's shoulders, now and then blinking blue winks. Did you never see a birdie blink a blue wink? This is how it first became a saying among the plains people. When a bird stands aloof watching your strange ways, a thin bluish white tissue slips quickly over his eyes and as quickly off again; so quick that you think it was only a mysterious blue wink. Sometimes when children grow drowsy they blink blue winks, while others who are too proud to look with friendly eyes upon people blink in this cold bird-manner.

The coyote was affected by both sleepiness and pride. His winks were almost as blue as the sky. In the midst of his new pleasure the swaying motion ceased. Iktomi had reached his dwelling place. The coyote felt drowsy no longer, for in the next instant he was slipping out of Iktomi's hands. He was falling, falling through space, and then he struck the ground with such a bump he did not wish to breathe for a while. He wondered what Iktomi would do, thus he lay still where he fell. Humming a dance-song, one from his bundle of mystery songs, Iktomi hopped and darted about at an imaginary dance and feast. He gathered dry willow sticks and broke them in two against his knee. He built a large fire out of doors. The flames leaped up high in red and yellow streaks. Now Iktomi returned to the coyote who had been looking on through his eyelashes.

Taking him again by his paws and hind feet, he swung him to and fro. Then as the wolf swung toward the red flames, Iktomi let him go. Once again the coyote fell through space. Hot air smote his nostrils. He saw red dancing fire, and now he struck a bed of cracking embers. With a quick turn he leaped out of the flames. From his heels were scattered a shower of red coals upon Iktomi's bare arms and shoulders. Dumfounded, Iktomi thought he saw a spirit walk out of his fire. His jaws fell apart. He thrust a palm to his face, hard over his mouth! He could scarce keep from shrieking.

Rolling over and over on the grass and rubbing the sides of his head against the ground, the coyote soon put out the fire on his fur. Iktomi's eyes were almost ready to jump out of his head as he stood cooling a burn on his brown arm with his breath.

Sitting on his haunches, on the opposite side of the fire from where Iktomi stood, the coyote began to laugh at him.

"Another day, my friend, do not take too much for granted. Make sure the enemy is stone dead before you make a fire!"

Then off he ran so swiftly that his long bushy tail hung out in a straight line with his back.

# IKTOMI AND THE FAWN

IN ONE OF his wanderings through the wooded lands, Iktomi saw a rare bird sitting high in a tree-top. Its long fan-like tail feathers had caught all the beautiful colors of the rainbow. Handsome in the glistening summer sun sat the bird of rainbow plumage. Iktomi hurried hither with his eyes fast on the bird.

He stood beneath the tree looking long and wistfully at the peacock's bright feathers. At length he heaved a sigh and began: "Oh, I wish I had such pretty feathers! How I wish I were not I! If only I were a handsome feathered creature how happy I would be! I'd be so glad to sit upon a very high tree and bask in the summer sun like you!" said he suddenly, pointing his bony finger up toward the peacock, who was eyeing the stranger below, turning his head from side to side.

"I beg of you make me into a bird with green and purple feathers like yours!" implored Iktomi, tired now of playing the brave in beaded buckskins. The peacock then spoke to Iktomi: "I have a magic power. My touch will change you in a moment into the most beautiful peacock if you can keep one condition."

"Yes! yes!" shouted Iktomi, jumping up and down, patting his lips with his palm, which caused his voice to vibrate in a peculiar fashion. "Yes! yes! I could keep ten conditions if only you would change me into a bird with long, bright tail feathers. Oh, I am so ugly! I am so tired of being myself! Change me! Do!"

Hereupon the peacock spread out both his wings, and scarce moving them, he sailed slowly down upon the ground. Right beside Iktomi he alighted. Very low in Iktomi's ear the peacock whispered, "Are you willing to keep one condition, though hard it be?"

"Yes! yes! I've told you ten of them if need be!" exclaimed Iktomi, with some impatience.

"Then I pronounce you a handsome feathered bird. No longer are you Iktomi the mischief-maker." Saying this the peacock touched Iktomi with the tips of his wings.

Iktomi vanished at the touch. There stood beneath the tree two handsome peacocks. While one of the pair strutted about with a head turned aside as if dazzled by his own bright-tinted tail feathers, the other bird soared slowly upward. He sat quiet and unconscious of his gay plumage. He seemed content to perch there on a large limb in the warm sunshine.

After a little while the vain peacock, dizzy with his bright colors, spread out his wings and lit on the same branch with the elder bird.

"Oh!" he exclaimed, "how hard to fly! Brightly tinted feathers are handsome, but I wish they were light enough to fly!" Just there the elder bird interrupted him. "That is the one condition. Never try to fly like other birds. Upon the day you try to fly you shall be changed into your former self."

"Oh, what a shame that bright feathers cannot fly into the sky!" cried the peacock. Already he grew restless. He longed to soar through space. He yearned to fly above the trees high upward to the sun.

"Oh, there I see a flock of birds flying thither! Oh! oh!" said he, flapping his wings, "I must try my wings! I am tired of bright tail feathers. I want to try my wings."

"No, no!" clucked the elder bird. The flock of chattering birds flew by with whirring wings. "Ōōp! ōōp!" called some to their mates.

Possessed by an irrepressible impulse the Iktomi peacock called out, "Hĕ! I want to come! Wait for me!" and with that he gave a lunge into the air. The flock of flying feathers wheeled about and lowered over the tree whence came the peacock's cry. Only one rare bird sat on the tree, and beneath, on the ground, stood a brave in brown buckskins.

"I am my old self again!" groaned Iktomi in a sad voice. "Make me over, pretty bird. Try me this once again!" he pleaded in vain.

"Old Iktomi wants to fly! Ah! We cannot wait for him!" sang the birds as they flew away.

Muttering unhappy vows to himself, Iktomi had not gone far when he chanced upon a bunch of long slender arrows. One by one they rose in the air and shot a straight line over the prairie.

Others shot up into the blue sky and were soon lost to sight. Only one was left. He was making ready for his flight when Iktomi rushed upon him and wailed, "I want to be an arrow! Make me into an arrow! I want to pierce the blue Blue overhead. I want to strike yonder summer sun in its center. Make me into an arrow!"

"Can you keep a condition? One condition, though hard it be?" the arrow turned to ask.

"Yes! Yes!" shouted Iktomi, delighted.

Hereupon the slender arrow tapped him gently with his sharp flint beak. There was no Iktomi, but two arrows stood ready to fly. "Now, young arrow, this is the one condition. Your flight must always be in a straight line. Never turn a curve nor jump about like a young fawn," said the arrow magician. He spoke slowly and sternly.

At once he set about to teach the new arrow how to shoot in a long straight line.

"This is the way to pierce the Blue overhead," said he; and off he spun high into the sky.

While he was gone a herd of deer came trotting by. Behind them played the young fawns together. They frolicked about like kittens. They bounced on all fours like balls. Then they pitched forward, kicking their heels in the air. The Iktomi arrow watched them so happy on the ground. Looking quickly up into the sky, he said in his heart, "The magician is out of sight. I'll just romp and frolic with these fawns until he returns. Fawns! Friends, do not fear me. I want to jump and leap with you. I long to be happy as you are," said he. The young fawns stopped with stiff legs and stared at the speaking arrow with large brown wondering eyes. "See! I can jump as well as you!" went on Iktomi. He gave one tiny leap like a fawn. All of a sudden the fawns snorted with extended nostrils at what they beheld. There among them stood Iktomi in brown buckskins, and the strange talking arrow was gone.

"Oh! I am myself. My old self!" cried Iktomi, pinching himself and plucking imaginary pieces out of his jacket.

"Hin-hin-hin! I wanted to fly!"

The real arrow now returned to the earth. He alighted very near Iktomi. From the high sky he had seen the fawns playing on the green. He had seen Iktomi make his one leap, and the charm was broken. Iktomi became his former self.

"Arrow, my friend, change me once more!" begged Iktomi.

"No, no more," replied the arrow. Then away he shot through the air in the direction his comrades had flown.

By this time the fawns gathered close around Iktomi. They poked their noses at him trying to know who he was.

Iktomi's tears were like a spring shower. A new desire dried them quickly away. Stepping boldly to the largest fawn, he looked closely at the little brown spots all over the furry face.

"Oh, fawn! What beautiful brown spots on your face! Fawn, dear little fawn, can you tell me how those brown spots were made on your face?"

"Yes," said the fawn. "When I was very, very small, my mother marked them on my face with a red hot fire. She dug a large hole in the ground and made a soft bed of grass and twigs in it. Then she placed me gently there. She covered me over with dry sweet grass and piled dry cedars on top. From a neighbor's fire she brought hither a red, red ember. This she tucked carefully in at my head. This is how the brown spots were made on my face."

"Now, fawn, my friend, will you do the same for me? Won't you mark my face with brown, brown spots just like yours?" asked Iktomi, always eager to be like other people.

"Yes. I can dig the ground and fill it with dry grass and sticks. If you will jump into the pit, I'll cover you with sweet smelling grass and cedar wood," answered the fawn.

"Say," interrupted Ikto, "will you be sure to cover me with a great deal of dry grass and twigs? You will make sure that the spots will be as brown as those you wear."

"Oh, yes. I'll pile up grass and willows once oftener than my mother did."

"Now let us dig the hole, pull the grass, and gather sticks," cried Iktomi in glee.

Thus with his own hands he aids in making his grave. After the hole was dug and cushioned with grass, Iktomi, muttering something about brown spots, leaped down into it. Lengthwise, flat on his back, he lay. While the fawn covered him over with cedars, a far-away voice came up through them, "Brown, brown spots to wear forever!" A red ember was tucked under the dry grass. Off scampered the fawns after their mothers; and when a great distance away they looked backward. They saw a blue smoke rising, writhing upward till it vanished in the blue ether.

"Is that Iktomi's spirit?" asked one fawn of another.

"No! I think he would jump out before he could burn into smoke and cinders," answered his comrade.

# THE BADGER AND THE BEAR

ON THE EDGE of a forest there lived a large family of badgers. In the ground their dwelling was made. Its walls and roof were covered with rocks and straw.

Old father badger was a great hunter. He knew well how to track the deer and buffalo. Every day he came home carrying on his back some wild game. This kept mother badger very busy, and the baby badgers very chubby. While the well-fed children played about, digging little make-believe dwellings, their mother hung thin sliced meats upon long willow racks. As fast as the meats were dried and seasoned by sun and wind, she packed them carefully away in a large thick bag.

This bag was like a huge stiff envelope, but far more beautiful to see, for it was painted all over with many bright colors. These firmly tied bags of dried meat were laid upon the rocks in the walls of the dwelling. In this way they were both useful and decorative.

One day father badger did not go off for a hunt. He stayed at home, making new arrows. His children sat about him on the ground floor. Their small black eyes danced with delight as they watched the gay colors painted upon the arrows.

All of a sudden there was heard a heavy footfall near the entrance way. The oval-shaped door-frame was pushed aside. In stepped a large black foot with great big claws. Then the other clumsy foot came next. All the while the baby badgers stared hard at the unexpected comer. After the second foot, in peeped the head of a big black bear! His black nose was dry and parched. Silently he entered the dwelling and sat down on the ground by the doorway. His black eyes never left the painted bags on the rocky walls. He guessed what was in them. He was a very hungry bear. Seeing the racks of red meat hanging in the yard, he had come to visit the badger family.

Though he was a stranger and his strong paws and jaws frightened the small badgers, the father said, "How, how, friend! Your lips and nose look feverish and hungry. Will you eat with us?"

"Yes, my friend," said the bear. "I am starved. I saw your racks of red fresh meat, and knowing your heart is kind, I came hither. Give me meat to eat, my friend."

Hereupon the mother badger took long strides across the room, and as she had to pass in front of the strange visitor, she said: "Ah han! Allow me to pass!" which was an apology.

"How, how!" replied the bear, drawing himself closer to the wall and crossing his shins together.

Mother badger chose the most tender red meat, and soon over a bed of coals she broiled the venison.

That day the bear had all he could eat. At nightfall he rose, and smacking his lips together,—that is the noisy way of saying "the food was very good!"—he left the badger dwelling. The baby badgers, peeping through the door-flap after the shaggy bear, saw him disappear into the woods near by.

Day after day the crackling of twigs in the forest told of heavy footsteps. Out would come the same black bear. He never lifted the door-flap, but thrusting it aside entered slowly in. Always in the same place by the entrance way he sat down with crossed shins.

His daily visits were so regular that mother badger placed a fur rug in his place. She did not wish a guest in her dwelling to sit upon the bare hard ground.

At last one time when the bear returned, his nose was bright and black. His coat was glossy. He had grown fat upon the badger's hospitality.

As he entered the dwelling a pair of wicked gleams shot out of his shaggy head. Surprised by the strange behavior of the guest who remained standing upon the rug, leaning his round back against the wall, father badger queried: "How, my friend! What?"

The bear took one stride forward and shook his paw in the badger's face. He said: "I am strong, very strong!"

"Yes, yes, so you are," replied the badger. From the farther end of the room mother badger muttered over her bead work: "Yes, you grew strong from our well-filled bowls."

The bear smiled, showing a row of large sharp teeth.

"I have no dwelling. I have no bags of dried meat. I have no arrows. All these I have found here on this spot," said he, stamping his heavy foot. "I want them! See! I am strong!" repeated he, lifting both his terrible paws.

Quietly the father badger spoke: "I fed you. I called you friend, though you came here a stranger and a beggar. For the sake of my little ones leave us in peace."

Mother badger, in her excited way, had pierced hard through the buckskin and stuck her fingers repeatedly with her sharp awl until she had laid aside her work. Now, while her husband was talking to the bear, she motioned with her hands to the children. On tiptoe they hastened to her side.

For reply came a low growl. It grew louder and more fierce. "Wä-ough!" he roared, and by force hurled the badgers out. First the father badger; then the mother. The little badgers he tossed by pairs. He threw them hard upon the ground. Standing in the entrance way and showing his ugly teeth, he snarled, "Be gone!"

The father and mother badger, having gained their feet, picked up their kicking little babes, and, wailing aloud, drew the air into their flattened lungs till they could stand alone upon their feet. No sooner had the baby badgers caught their breath than they howled and shrieked with pain and fright. Ah! what a dismal cry was theirs as the whole badger family went forth wailing from out their own dwelling! A little distance away from their stolen house the father badger built a small round hut. He made it of bent willows and covered it with dry grass and twigs.

This was shelter for the night; but alas! it was empty of food and arrows. All day father badger prowled through the forest, but without his arrows he could not get food for his children. Upon his return, the cry of the little ones for meat, the sad quiet of the mother with bowed head, hurt him like a poisoned arrow wound.

"I'll beg meat for you!" said he in an unsteady voice. Covering his head and entire body in a long loose robe he halted beside the big black bear. The bear was slicing red meat to hang upon the rack. He did not pause for a look at the comer. As the badger stood there unrecognized, he saw that the bear had brought with him his whole family. Little cubs played under the high-hanging new meats. They laughed and pointed with their wee noses upward at the thin sliced meats upon the poles.

"Have you no heart, Black Bear? My children are starving. Give me a small piece of meat for them," begged the badger.

"Wä-ough!" growled the angry bear, and pounced upon the badger. "Be gone!" said he, and with his big hind foot he sent father badger sprawling on the ground.

All the little ruffian bears hooted and shouted "ha-ha!" to see the beggar fall upon his face. There was one, however, who did not even smile. He was the youngest cub. His fur coat was not as black and glossy as those his elders wore. The hair was dry and dingy. It looked much more like kinky wool. He was the ugly cub. Poor little baby bear! he had always been laughed at by his older brothers. He could not help being himself. He could not change the differences between himself and his brothers. Thus again, though the rest laughed aloud at the badger's fall, he did not see the joke. His face was long and earnest. In his heart he was sad to see the badgers crying and starving. In his breast spread a burning desire to share his food with them.

"I shall not ask my father for meat to give away. He would say 'No!' Then my brothers would laugh at me," said the ugly baby bear to himself.

In an instant, as if his good intention had passed from him, he was singing happily and skipping around his father at work. Singing in his small high voice and dragging his feet in long strides after him, as if a prankish spirit oozed out from his heels, he strayed off through the tall grass. He was ambling toward the small round hut. When directly in front of the entrance way, he made a quick side kick with his left hind leg. Lo! there fell into the badger's hut a piece of fresh meat. It was tough meat, full of sinews, yet it was the only piece he could take without his father's notice.

Thus having given meat to the hungry badgers, the ugly baby bear ran quickly away to his father again.

On the following day the father badger came back once more. He stood watching the big bear cutting thin slices of meat.

"Give—" he began, when the bear, turning upon him with a growl, thrust him cruelly aside. The badger fell on his hands. He fell where the grass was wet with the blood of the newly carved buffalo. His keen starving eyes caught sight of a little red clot lying bright upon the green. Looking fearfully toward the bear and seeing his head was turned away, he snatched up the small thick blood. Underneath his girdled blanket he hid it in his hand.

On his return to his family, he said within himself: "I'll pray the Great Spirit to bless it." Thus he built a small round lodge.

Sprinkling water upon the heated heap of sacred stones within, he made ready to purge his body. "The buffalo blood, too, must be purified before I ask a blessing upon it," thought the badger. He carried it into the sacred vapor lodge. After placing it near the sacred stones, he sat down beside it. After a long silence, he muttered: "Great Spirit, bless this little buffalo blood." Then he arose, and with a quiet dignity stepped out of the lodge. Close behind him some one followed. The badger turned to look over his shoulder and to his great joy he beheld a Dakota brave in handsome buckskins. In his hand he carried a magic arrow. Across his back dangled a long fringed quiver. In answer to the badger's prayer, the avenger had sprung from out of the red globules.

"My son!" exclaimed the badger with extended right hand.

"How, father," replied the brave; "I am your avenger!"

Immediately the badger told the sad story of his hungry little ones and the stingy bear.

Listening closely, the young man stood looking steadily upon the ground.

At length the father badger moved away.

"Where?" queried the avenger.

"My son, we have no food. I am going again to beg for meat," answered the badger.

"Then I go with you," replied the young brave. This made the old badger happy. He was proud of his son. He was delighted to be called "father" by the first human creature.

The bear saw the badger coming in the distance. He narrowed his eyes at the tall stranger walking beside him. He spied the arrow. At once he guessed it was the avenger of whom he had heard long, long ago. As they approached, the bear stood erect with a hand on his thigh. He smiled upon them.

"How, badger, my friend! Here is my knife. Cut your favorite pieces from the deer," said he, holding out a long thin blade.

"How!" said the badger eagerly. He wondered what had inspired the big bear to such a generous deed. The young avenger waited till the badger took the long knife in his hand.

Gazing full into the black bear's face, he said: "I come to do justice. You have returned only a knife to my poor father. Now return to him his dwelling." His voice was deep and powerful. In his black eyes burned a steady fire.

The long strong teeth of the bear rattled against each other, and his shaggy body shook with fear. "Ahōw!" cried he, as if he had been shot. Running into the dwelling he gasped, breathless and trembling, "Come out, all of you! This is the badger's dwelling. We must flee to the forest for fear of the avenger who carries the magic arrow."

Out they hurried, all the bears, and disappeared into the woods.

Singing and laughing, the badgers returned to their own dwelling.

Then the avenger left them.

"I go," said he in parting, "over the earth."

# THE TREE-BOUND

IT WAS A clear summer day. The blue, blue sky dropped low over the edge of the green level land. A large yellow sun hung directly overhead.

The singing of birds filled the summer space between earth and sky with sweet music. Again and again sang a yellow-breasted birdie—"Koda Ni Dakota!" He insisted upon it. "Koda Ni Dakota!" which was "Friend, you're a Dakota! Friend, you're a Dakota!" Perchance the birdie meant the avenger with the magic arrow, for there across the plain he strode. He was handsome in his paint and feathers, proud with his great buckskin quiver on his back and a long bow in his hand. Afar to an eastern camp of cone-shaped teepees he was going. There over the Indian village hovered a large red eagle threatening the safety of the people. Every morning rose this terrible red bird out of a high chalk bluff and spreading out his gigantic wings soared slowly over the round camp ground. Then it was that the people, terror-stricken, ran screaming into their lodges. Covering their heads with their blankets, they sat trembling with fear. No one dared to venture out till the red eagle had disappeared beyond the west, where meet the blue and green.

In vain tried the chieftain of the tribe to find among his warriors a powerful marksman who could send a death arrow to the man-hungry bird. At last to urge his men to their utmost skill he bade his crier proclaim a new reward.

Of the chieftain's two beautiful daughters he would have his choice who brought the dreaded red eagle with an arrow in its breast.

Upon hearing these words, the men of the village, both young and old, both heroes and cowards, trimmed new arrows for the contest. At gray dawn there stood indistinct under the shadow of

115

the bluff many human figures; silent as ghosts and wrapped in robes girdled tight about their waists, they waited with chosen bow and arrow.

Some cunning old warriors stayed not with the group. They crouched low upon the open ground. But all eyes alike were fixed upon the top of the high bluff. Breathless they watched for the soaring of the red eagle.

From within the dwellings many eyes peeped through the small holes in the front lapels of the teepee. With shaking knees and hard-set teeth, the women peered out upon the Dakota men prowling about with bows and arrows.

At length when the morning sun also peeped over the eastern horizon at the armed Dakotas, the red eagle walked out upon the edge of the cliff. Pluming his gorgeous feathers, he ruffled his neck and flapped his strong wings together. Then he dived into the air. Slowly he winged his way over the round camp ground; over the men with their strong bows and arrows! In an instant the long bows were bent. Strong straight arrows with red feathered tips sped upward to the blue sky. Ah! slowly moved those indifferent wings, untouched by the poison-beaked arrows. Off to the west beyond the reach of arrow, beyond the reach of eye, the red eagle flew away.

A sudden clamor of high-pitched voices broke the deadly stillness of the dawn. The women talked excitedly about the invulnerable red of the eagle's feathers, while the would-be heroes sulked within their wigwams. "Hĕ-hĕ-hĕ!" groaned the chieftain.

On the evening of the same day sat a group of hunters around a bright burning fire. They were talking of a strange young man whom they spied while out upon a hunt for deer beyond the bluffs. They saw the stranger taking aim. Following the point of his arrow with their eyes, they beheld a herd of buffalo. The arrow sprang from the bow! It darted into the skull of the foremost buffalo. But unlike other arrows it pierced through the head of the creature and spinning in the air lit into the next buffalo head. One by one the buffalo fell upon the sweet grass they were grazing. With straight quivering limbs they lay on their sides. The young man stood calmly by, counting on his fingers the buffalo as they dropped dead to the ground. When the last one fell, he ran thither and picking up his magic arrow wiped it carefully on the soft grass. He slipped it into his long fringed quiver.

"He is going to make a feast for some hungry tribe of men or beasts!" cried the hunters among themselves as they hastened away.

They were afraid of the stranger with the sacred arrow. When the hunter's tale of the stranger's arrow reached the ears of the chieftain, his face brightened with a smile. He sent forth fleet horsemen, to learn of him his birth, his name, and his deeds.

"If he is the avenger with the magic arrow, sprung up from the earth out of a clot of buffalo blood, bid him come hither. Let him kill the red eagle with his magic arrow. Let him win for himself one of my beautiful daughters," he had said to his messengers, for the old story of the badger's man-son was known all over the level lands.

After four days and nights the braves returned. "He is coming," they said. "We have seen him. He is straight and tall; handsome in face, with large black eyes. He paints his round cheeks with bright red, and wears the penciled lines of red over his temples like our men of honored rank. He carries on his back a long fringed quiver in which he keeps his magic arrow. His bow is long and strong. He is coming now to kill the big red eagle." All around the camp ground from mouth to ear passed those words of the returned messengers.

Now it chanced that immortal Iktomi, fully recovered from the brown burnt spots, overheard the people talking. At once he was filled with a new desire. "If only I had the magic arrow, I would kill the red eagle and win the chieftain's daughter for a wife," said he in his heart.

Back to his lonely wigwam he hastened. Beneath the tree in front of his teepee he sat upon the ground with chin between his drawn-up knees. His keen eyes scanned the wide plain. He was watching for the avenger.

"'He is coming!' said the people," muttered old Iktomi. All of a sudden he raised an open palm to his brow and peered afar into the west. The summer sun hung bright in the middle of a cloudless sky. There across the green prairie was a man walking bareheaded toward the east.

"Ha! ha! 'tis he! the man with the magic arrow!" laughed Iktomi. And when the bird with the yellow breast sang loud again—"Koda Ni Dakota! Friend, you're a Dakota!"—Iktomi put his hand over his mouth as he threw his head far backward, laughing at both the bird and man.

"He is your friend, but his arrow will kill one of your kind! He is a Dakota, but soon he'll grow into the bark on this tree! Ha! ha! ha!" he laughed again.

The young avenger walked with swaying strides nearer and nearer toward the lonely wigwam and tree. Iktomi heard the swish! swish! of the stranger's feet through the tall grass. He was passing now beyond the tree, when Iktomi, springing to his feet, called out: "How, how, my friend! I see you are dressed in handsome deerskins and have red paint on your cheeks. You are going to some feast or dance, may I ask?" Seeing the young man only smiled Iktomi went on: "I have not had a mouthful of food this day. Have pity on me, young brave, and shoot yonder bird for me!" With these words Iktomi pointed toward the tree-top, where sat a bird on the highest branch. The young avenger, always ready to help those in distress, sent an arrow upward and the bird fell. In the next branch it was caught between the forked prongs.

"My friend, climb the tree and get the bird. I cannot climb so high. I would get dizzy and fall," pleaded Iktomi. The avenger began to scale the tree, when Iktomi cried to him: "My friend, your beaded buckskins may be torn by the branches. Leave them safe upon the grass till you are down again."

"You are right," replied the young man, quickly slipping off his long fringed quiver. Together with his dangling pouches and tinkling ornaments, he placed it on the ground. Now he climbed the tree unhindered. Soon from the top he took the bird. "My friend, toss to me your arrow that I may have the honor of wiping it clean on soft deerskin!" exclaimed Iktomi.

"How!" said the brave, and threw the bird and arrow to the ground.

At once Iktomi seized the arrow. Rubbing it first on the grass and then on a piece of deerskin, he muttered indistinct words all the while. The young man, stepping downward from limb to limb, hearing the low muttering, said: "Iktomi, I cannot hear what you say!"

"Oh, my friend, I was only talking of your big heart."

Again stooping over the arrow Iktomi continued his repetition of charm words. "Grow fast, grow fast to the bark of the tree," he whispered. Still the young man moved slowly downward. Suddenly dropping the arrow and standing erect, Iktomi said aloud: "Grow fast to the bark of the tree!" Before the brave could leap from the tree he became tight-grown to the bark.

"Ah! ha!" laughed the bad Iktomi. "I have the magic arrow! I have the beaded buckskins of the great avenger!" Hooting and dancing beneath the tree, he said: "I shall kill the red eagle; I shall wed the chieftain's beautiful daughter!"

"Oh, Iktomi, set me free!" begged the tree-bound Dakota brave. But Iktomi's ears were like the fungus on a tree. He did not hear with them.

Wearing the handsome buckskins and carrying proudly the magic arrow in his right hand, he started off eastward. Imitating the swaying strides of the avenger, he walked away with a face turned slightly skyward.

"Oh, set me free! I am glued to the tree like its own bark! Cut me loose!" moaned the prisoner.

A young woman, carrying on her strong back a bundle of tightly bound willow sticks, passed near by the lonely teepee. She heard the wailing man's voice. She paused to listen to the sad words. Looking around she saw nowhere a human creature. "It may be a spirit," thought she.

"Oh! cut me loose! set me free! Iktomi has played me false! He has made me bark of his tree!" cried the voice again.

The young woman dropped her pack of firewood to the ground. With her stone axe she hurried to the tree. There before her astonished eyes clung a young brave close to the tree.

Too shy for words, yet too kind-hearted to leave the stranger tree-bound, she cut loose the whole bark. Like an open jacket she drew it to the ground. With it came the young man also. Free once more, he started away. Looking backward, a few paces from the young woman, he waved his hand, upward and downward, before her face. This was a sign of gratitude used when words failed to interpret strong emotion.

When the bewildered woman reached her dwelling, she mounted a pony and rode swiftly across the rolling land. To the camp ground in the east, to the chieftain troubled by the red eagle, she carried her story.

# SHOOTING OF THE RED EAGLE

A MAN IN buckskins sat upon the top of a little hillock. The setting sun shone bright upon a strong bow in his hand. His face was turned toward the round camp ground at the foot of the hill. He had walked a long journey hither. He was waiting for the chieftain's men to spy him.

Soon four strong men ran forth from the center wigwam toward the hillock, where sat the man with the long bow.

"He is the avenger come to shoot the red eagle," cried the runners to each other as they bent forward swinging their elbows together.

They reached the side of the stranger, but he did not heed them. Proud and silent he gazed upon the cone-shaped wigwams beneath him. Spreading a handsomely decorated buffalo robe before the man, two of the warriors lifted him by each shoulder and placed him gently on it. Then the four men took, each, a corner of the blanket and carried the stranger, with long proud steps, toward the chieftain's teepee.

Ready to greet the stranger, the tall chieftain stood at the entrance way. "How, you are the avenger with the magic arrow!" said he, extending to him a smooth soft hand.

"How, great chieftain!" replied the man, holding long the chieftain's hand. Entering the teepee, the chieftain motioned the young man to the right side of the doorway, while he sat down opposite him with a center fire burning between them. Wordless, like a bashful Indian maid, the avenger ate in silence the food set before him on the ground in front of his crossed shins. When he had finished his meal he handed the empty bowl to the chieftain's wife, saying, "Mother-in-law, here is your dish!"

"Han, my son!" answered the woman, taking the bowl.

With the magic arrow in his quiver the stranger felt not in the least too presuming in addressing the woman as his mother-in-law.

Complaining of fatigue, he covered his face with his blanket and soon within the chieftain's teepee he lay fast asleep.

"The young man is not handsome after all!" whispered the woman in her husband's ear.

"Ah, but after he has killed the red eagle he will seem handsome enough!" answered the chieftain.

That night the star men in their burial procession in the sky reached the low northern horizon, before the center fires within the teepees had flickered out. The ringing laughter which had floated up through the smoke lapels was now hushed, and only the distant howling of wolves broke the quiet of the village. But the lull between midnight and dawn was short indeed. Very early the oval-shaped door-flaps were thrust aside and many brown faces peered out of the wigwams toward the top of the highest bluff.

Now the sun rose up out of the east. The red painted avenger stood ready within the camp ground for the flying of the red eagle. He appeared, that terrible bird! He hovered over the round village as if he could pounce down upon it and devour the whole tribe.

When the first arrow shot up into the sky the anxious watchers thrust a hand quickly over their half-uttered "hinnu!" The second and the third arrows flew upward but missed by a wide space the red eagle soaring with lazy indifference over the little man with the long bow. All his arrows he spent in vain. "Ah! my blanket brushed my elbow and shifted the course of my arrow!" said the stranger as the people gathered around him.

During this happening, a woman on horseback halted her pony at the chieftain's teepee. It was no other than the young woman who cut loose the tree-bound captive!

While she told the story the chieftain listened with downcast face. "I passed him on my way. He is near!" she ended.

Indignant at the bold impostor, the wrathful eyes of the chieftain snapped fire like red cinders in the night time. His lips were closed. At length to the woman he said: "How, you have done me a good deed." Then with quick decision he gave command to a fleet horseman to meet the avenger. "Clothe him in these my best buckskins," said he, pointing to a bundle within the wigwam.

In the meanwhile strong men seized Iktomi and dragged him by his long hair to the hilltop. There upon a mock-pillared grave they bound him hand and feet. Grown-ups and children sneered and hooted at Iktomi's disgrace. For a half-day he lay there, the laughing-stock of the people. Upon the arrival of the real avenger, Iktomi was released and chased away beyond the outer limits of the camp ground.

On the following morning at daybreak, peeped the people out of half-open door-flaps.

There again in the midst of the large camp ground was a man in beaded buckskins. In his hand was a strong bow and red-tipped arrow. Again the big red eagle appeared on the edge of the bluff. He plumed his feathers and flapped his huge wings.

The young man crouched low to the ground. He placed the arrow on the bow, drawing a poisoned flint for the eagle.

The bird rose into the air. He moved his outspread wings one, two, three times and lo! the eagle tumbled from the great height and fell heavily to the earth. An arrow stuck in his breast! He was dead!

So quick was the hand of the avenger, so sure his sight, that no one had seen the arrow fly from his long bent bow.

In awe and amazement the village was dumb. And when the avenger, plucking a red eagle feather, placed it in his black hair, a loud shout of the people went up to the sky. Then hither and thither ran singing men and women making a great feast for the avenger.

Thus he won the beautiful Indian princess who never tired of telling to her children the story of the big red eagle.

# IKTOMI AND THE TURTLE

The huntsman Patkaša (turtle) stood bent over a newly slain deer.

The red-tipped arrow he drew from the wounded deer was unlike the arrows in his own quiver. Another's stray shot had killed the deer. Patkasa had hunted all the morning without so much as spying an ordinary blackbird.

At last returning homeward, tired and heavy-hearted that he had no meat for the hungry mouths in his wigwam, he walked slowly with downcast eyes. Kind ghosts pitied the unhappy hunter and led him to the newly slain deer, that his children should not cry for food.

When Patkasa stumbled upon the deer in his path, he exclaimed: "Good spirits have pushed me hither!"

Thus he leaned long over the gift of the friendly ghosts.

"How, my friend!" said a voice behind his ear, and a hand fell on his shoulder. It was not a spirit this time. It was old Iktomi.

"How, Iktomi!" answered Patkasa, still stooping over the deer.

"My friend, you are a skilled hunter," began Iktomi, smiling a thin smile which spread from one ear to the other.

Suddenly raising up his head Patkasa's black eyes twinkled as he asked: "Oh, you really say so?"

"Yes, my friend, you are a skillful fellow. Now let us have a little contest. Let us see who can jump over the deer without touching a hair on his hide," suggested Iktomi.

"Oh, I fear I cannot do it!" cried Patkasa, rubbing his funny, thick palms together.

"Have no coward's doubt, Patkasa. I say you are a skillful fellow who finds nothing hard to do." With these words Iktomi led Patkasa a short distance away. In little puffs Patkasa laughed uneasily.

"Now, you may jump first," said Iktomi.

Patkasa, with doubled fists, swung his fat arms to and fro, all the while biting hard his under lip.

Just before the run and leap Iktomi put in: "Let the winner have the deer to eat!"

It was too late now to say no. Patkasa was more afraid of being called a coward than of losing the deer. "Ho-wo," he replied, still working his short arms. At length he started off on the run. So quick and small were his steps that he seemed to be kicking the ground only. Then the leap! But Patkasa tripped upon a stick and fell hard against the side of the deer.

"Hĕ-hĕ-hĕ!" exclaimed Iktomi, pretending disappointment that his friend had fallen.

Lifting him to his feet, he said: "Now it is my turn to try the high jump!" Hardly was the last word spoken than Iktomi gave a leap high above the deer.

"The game is mine!" laughed he, patting the sullen Patkasa on the back. "My friend, watch the deer while I go to bring my children," said Iktomi, darting lightly through the tall grass.

Patkasa was always ready to believe the words of scheming people and to do the little favors any one asked of him. However, on this occasion, he did not answer "Yes, my friend." He realized that Iktomi's flattering tongue had made him foolish.

He turned up his nose at Iktomi, now almost out of sight, as much as to say: "Oh, no, Ikto; I do not hear your words!"

Soon there came a murmur of voices. The sound of laughter grew louder and louder. All of a sudden it became hushed. Old Iktomi led his young Iktomi brood to the place where he had left the turtle, but it was vacant. Nowhere was there any sign of Patkasa or the deer. Then the babes did howl!

"Be still!" said father Iktomi to his children. "I know where Patkasa lives. Follow me. I shall take you to the turtle's dwelling." He ran along a narrow footpath toward the creek near by. Close upon his heels came his children with tear-streaked faces.

"There!" said Iktomi in a loud whisper as he gathered his little ones on the bank. "There is Patkasa broiling venison! There is his teepee, and the savory fire is in his front yard!"

The young Iktomis stretched their necks and rolled their round black eyes like newly hatched birds. They peered into the water.

"Now, I will cool Patkasa's fire. I shall bring you the broiled venison. Watch closely. When you see the black coals rise to the surface of the water, clap your hands and shout aloud, for soon after that sign I shall return to you with some tender meat."

Thus saying Iktomi plunged into the creek. Splash! splash! the water leaped upward into spray. Scarcely had it become leveled and smooth than there bubbled up many black spots. The creek was seething with the dancing of round black things.

"The cooled fire! The coals!" laughed the brood of Iktomis. Clapping together their little hands, they chased one another along the edge of the creek. They shouted and hooted with great glee.

"Āhäs!" said a gruff voice across the water. It was Patkasa. In a large willow tree leaning far over the water he sat upon a large limb. On the very same branch was a bright burning fire over which Patkasa broiled the venison. By this time the water was calm again. No more danced those black spots on its surface, for they were the toes of old Iktomi. He was drowned.

The Iktomi children hurried away from the creek, crying and calling for their water-dead father.

# DANCE IN A BUFFALO SKULL

IT WAS NIGHT upon the prairie. Overhead the stars were twinkling bright their red and yellow lights. The moon was young. A silvery thread among the stars, it soon drifted low beneath the horizon.

Upon the ground the land was pitchy black. There are night people on the plain who love the dark. Amid the black level land they meet to frolic under the stars. Then when their sharp ears hear any strange footfalls nigh they scamper away into the deep shadows of night. There they are safely hid from all dangers, they think.

Thus it was that one very black night, afar off from the edge of the level land, out of the wooded river bottom glided forth two balls of fire. They came farther and farther into the level land. They grew larger and brighter. The dark hid the body of the creature with those fiery eyes. They came on and on, just over the tops of the prairie grass. It might have been a wildcat prowling low on soft, stealthy feet. Slowly but surely the terrible eyes drew nearer and nearer to the heart of the level land.

There in a huge old buffalo skull was a gay feast and dance! Tiny little field mice were singing and dancing in a circle to the boom-boom of a wee, wee drum. They were laughing and talking among themselves while their chosen singers sang loud a merry tune.

They built a small open fire within the center of their queer dance house. The light streamed out of the buffalo skull through all the curious sockets and holes.

A light on the plain in the middle of the night was an unusual thing. But so merry were the mice they did not hear the "kinš, kinš" of sleepy birds, disturbed by the unaccustomed fire.

A pack of wolves, fearing to come nigh this night fire, stood together a little distance away, and, turning their pointed noses to the stars, howled and yelped most dismally. Even the cry of the wolves was unheeded by the mice within the lighted buffalo skull.

They were feasting and dancing; they were singing and laughing—those funny little furry fellows.

All the while across the dark from out the low river bottom came that pair of fiery eyes.

Now closer and more swift, now fiercer and glaring, the eyes moved toward the buffalo skull. All unconscious of those fearful eyes, the happy mice nibbled at dried roots and venison. The singers had started another song. The drummers beat the time, turning their heads from side to side in rhythm. In a ring around the fire hopped the mice, each bouncing hard on his two hind feet. Some carried their tails over their arms, while others trailed them proudly along.

Ah, very near are those round yellow eyes! Very low to the ground they seem to creep—creep toward the buffalo skull. All of a sudden they slide into the eye-sockets of the old skull.

"Spirit of the buffalo!" squeaked a frightened mouse as he jumped out from a hole in the back part of the skull.

"A cat! a cat!" cried other mice as they scrambled out of holes both large and snug. Noiseless they ran away into the dark.

# THE TOAD AND THE BOY

THE WATER-FOWLS WERE flying over the marshy lakes. It was now the hunting season. Indian men, with bows and arrows, were wading waist deep amid the wild rice. Near by, within their wigwams, the wives were roasting wild duck and making down pillows.

In the largest teepee sat a young mother wrapping red porcupine quills about the long fringes of a buckskin cushion. Beside her lay a black-eyed baby boy cooing and laughing. Reaching and kicking upward with his tiny hands and feet, he played with the dangling strings of his heavy-beaded bonnet hanging empty on a tent pole above him.

At length the mother laid aside her red quills and white sinew-threads. The babe fell fast asleep. Leaning on one hand and softly whispering a little lullaby, she threw a light cover over her baby. It was almost time for the return of her husband.

Remembering there were no willow sticks for the fire, she quickly girdled her blanket tight about her waist, and with a short-handled ax slipped through her belt, she hurried away toward the wooded ravine. She was strong and swung an ax as skillfully as any man. Her loose buckskin dress was made for such freedom. Soon carrying easily a bundle of long willows on her back, with a loop of rope over both her shoulders, she came striding homeward.

Near the entrance way she stooped low, at once shifting the bundle to the right and with both hands lifting the noose from over her head. Having thus dropped the wood to the ground, she disappeared into her teepee. In a moment she came running out again, crying, "My son! My little son is gone!" Her keen eyes swept east and west and all around her. There was nowhere any sign of the child.

Running with clinched fists to the nearest teepees, she called: "Has any one seen my baby? He is gone! My little son is gone!"

"Hinnú! Hinnú!" exclaimed the women, rising to their feet and rushing out of their wigwams.

"We have not seen your child! What has happened?" queried the women.

With great tears in her eyes the mother told her story.

"We will search with you," they said to her as she started off.

They met the returning husbands, who turned about and joined in the hunt for the missing child. Along the shore of the lakes, among the high-grown reeds, they looked in vain. He was nowhere to be found. After many days and nights the search was given up. It was sad, indeed, to hear the mother wailing aloud for her little son.

It was growing late in the autumn. The birds were flying high toward the south. The teepees around the lakes were gone, save one lonely dwelling.

Till the winter snow covered the ground and ice covered the lakes, the wailing woman's voice was heard from that solitary wigwam. From some far distance was also the sound of the father's voice singing a sad song.

Thus ten summers and as many winters have come and gone since the strange disappearance of the little child. Every autumn with the hunters came the unhappy parents of the lost baby to search again for him.

Toward the latter part of the tenth season when, one by one, the teepees were folded and the families went away from the lake region, the mother walked again along the lake shore weeping. One evening, across the lake from where the crying woman stood, a pair of bright black eyes peered at her through the tall reeds and wild rice. A little wild boy stopped his play among the tall grasses. His long, loose hair hanging down his brown back and shoulders was carelessly tossed from his round face. He wore a loin cloth of woven sweet grass. Crouching low to the marshy ground, he listened to the wailing voice. As the voice grew hoarse and only sobs shook the slender figure of the woman, the eyes of the wild boy grew dim and wet.

At length, when the moaning ceased, he sprang to his feet and ran like a nymph with swift outstretched toes. He rushed into a small hut of reeds and grasses.

"Mother! Mother! Tell me what voice it was I heard which pleased my ears, but made my eyes grow wet!" said he, breathless.

"Han, my son," grunted a big, ugly toad. "It was the voice of a weeping woman you heard. My son, do not say you like it. Do not tell me it brought tears to your eyes. You have never heard me weep. I can please your ear and break your heart. Listen!" replied the great old toad.

Stepping outside, she stood by the entrance way. She was old and badly puffed out. She had reared a large family of little toads, but none of them had aroused her love, nor ever grieved her. She had heard the wailing human voice and marveled at the throat which produced the strange sound. Now, in her great desire to keep the stolen boy awhile longer, she ventured to cry as the Dakota woman does. In a gruff, coarse voice she broke forth:

"Hin-hin, doe-skin! Hin-hin, Ermine, Ermine! Hin-hin, red blanket, with white border!"

Not knowing that the syllables of a Dakota's cry are the names of loved ones gone, the ugly toad mother sought to please the boy's ear with the names of valuable articles. Having shrieked in a torturing voice and mouthed extravagant names, the old toad rolled her tearless eyes with great satisfaction. Hopping back into her dwelling, she asked:

"My son, did my voice bring tears to your eyes? Did my words bring gladness to your ears? Do you not like my wailing better?"

"No, no!" pouted the boy with some impatience. "I want to hear the woman's voice! Tell me, mother, why the human voice stirs all my feelings!"

The toad mother said within her breast, "The human child has heard and seen his real mother. I cannot keep him longer, I fear. Oh, no, I cannot give away the pretty creature I have taught to call me 'mother' all these many winters."

"Mother," went on the child voice, "tell me one thing. Tell me why my little brothers and sisters are all unlike me."

The big, ugly toad, looking at her pudgy children, said: "The eldest is always best."

This reply quieted the boy for a while. Very closely watched the old toad mother her stolen human son. When by chance he started off alone, she shoved out one of her own children after him, saying: "Do not come back without your big brother."

Thus the wild boy with the long, loose hair sits every day on a marshy island hid among the tall reeds. But he is not alone. Always at his feet hops a little toad brother. One day an Indian hunter, wading in the deep waters, spied the boy. He had heard of the baby stolen long ago.

"This is he!" murmured the hunter to himself as he ran to his wigwam. "I saw among the tall reeds a black-haired boy at play!" shouted he to the people.

At once the unhappy father and mother cried out, "'Tis he, our boy!" Quickly he led them to the lake. Peeping through the wild rice, he pointed with unsteady finger toward the boy playing all unawares.

"'Tis he! 'tis he!" cried the mother, for she knew him.

In silence the hunter stood aside, while the happy father and mother caressed their baby boy grown tall.

# IYA, THE CAMP-EATER

FROM THE TALL grass came the voice of a crying babe. The hunts-men who were passing nigh heard and halted.

The tallest one among them hastened toward the high grass with long, cautious strides. He waded through the growth of green with just a head above it all. Suddenly exclaiming "Hunhe!" he dropped out of sight. In another instant he held up in both his hands a tiny little baby, wrapped in soft brown buckskins.

"Oh ho, a wood-child!" cried the men, for they were hunting along the wooded river bottom where this babe was found.

While the hunters were questioning whether or no they should carry it home, the wee Indian baby kept up his little howl.

"His voice is strong!" said one.

"At times it sounds like an old man's voice!" whispered a super-stitious fellow, who feared some bad spirit hid in the small child to cheat them by and by.

"Let us take it to our wise chieftain," at length they said; and the moment they started toward the camp ground the strange wood-child ceased to cry.

Beside the chieftain's teepee waited the hunters while the tall man entered with the child.

"How! how!" nodded the kind-faced chieftain, listening to the queer story. Then rising, he took the infant in his strong arms; gently he laid the black-eyed babe in his daughter's lap. "This is to be your little son!" said he, smiling.

"Yes, father," she replied. Pleased with the child, she smoothed the long black hair fringing his round brown face.

"Tell the people that I give a feast and dance this day for the naming of my daughter's little son," bade the chieftain.

In the meanwhile among the men waiting by the entrance way, one said in a low voice: "I have heard that bad spirits come as little children into a camp which they mean to destroy."

"No! no! Let us not be overcautious. It would be cowardly to leave a baby in the wild wood where prowl the hungry wolves!" answered an elderly man.

The tall man now came out of the chieftain's teepee. With a word he sent them to their dwellings half running with joy.

"A feast! a dance for the naming of the chieftain's grandchild!" cried he in a loud voice to the village people.

"What? what?" asked they in great surprise, holding a hand to the ear to catch the words of the crier.

There was a momentary silence among the people while they listened to the ringing voice of the man walking in the center ground. Then broke forth a rippling, laughing babble among the cone-shaped teepees. All were glad to hear of the chieftain's grandson. They were happy to attend the feast and dance for its naming. With excited fingers they twisted their hair into glossy braids and painted their cheeks with bright red paint. To and fro hurried the women, handsome in their gala-day dress. Men in loose deerskins, with long tinkling metal fringes, strode in small numbers toward the center of the round camp ground.

Here underneath a temporary shade-house of green leaves they were to dance and feast. The children in deerskins and paints, just like their elders, were jolly little men and women. Beside their eager parents they skipped along toward the green dance house.

Here seated in a large circle, the people were assembled, the proud chieftain rose with the little baby in his arms. The noisy hum of voices was hushed. Not a tinkling of a metal fringe broke the silence. The crier came forward to greet the chieftain, then bent attentively over the small babe, listening to the words of the chieftain. When he paused the crier spoke aloud to the people:

"This woodland child is adopted by the chieftain's eldest daughter. His name is Chaske. He wears the title of the eldest son. In honor of Chaske the chieftain gives this feast and dance! These are the words of him you see holding a baby in his arms."

"Yes! Yes! Hinnu! How!" came from the circle. At once the drummers beat softly and slowly their drum while the chosen singers hummed together to find the common pitch. The beat of the drum grew louder and faster. The singers burst forth in a lively tune. Then the drumbeats subsided and faintly marked the rhythm of the singing. Here and there bounced up men and women, both young and old. They danced and sang with merry light hearts. Then came the hour of feasting.

Late into the night the air of the camp ground was alive with the laughing voices of women and the singing in unison of young men. Within her father's teepee sat the chieftain's daughter. Proud of her little one, she watched over him asleep in her lap.

Gradually a deep quiet stole over the camp ground, as one by one the people fell into pleasant dreams. Now all the village was still. Alone sat the beautiful young mother watching the babe in her lap, asleep with a gaping little mouth. Amid the quiet of the night, her ear heard the far-off hum of many voices. The faint sound of murmuring people was in the air. Upward she glanced at the smoke hole of the wigwam and saw a bright star peeping down upon her. "Spirits in the air above?" she wondered. Yet there was no sign to tell her of their nearness. The fine small sound of voices grew larger and nearer.

"Father! rise! I hear the coming of some tribe. Hostile or friendly—I cannot tell. Rise and see!" whispered the young woman.

"Yes, my daughter!" answered the chieftain, springing to his feet.

Though asleep, his ear was ever alert. Thus rushing out into the open, he listened for strange sounds. With an eagle eye he scanned the camp ground for some sign.

Returning he said: "My daughter, I hear nothing and see no sign of evil nigh."

"Oh! the sound of many voices comes up from the earth about me!" exclaimed the young mother.

Bending low over her babe she gave ear to the ground. Horrified was she to find the mysterious sound came out of the open mouth of her sleeping child!

"Why so unlike other babes!" she cried within her heart as she slipped him gently from her lap to the ground. "Mother, listen and tell me if this child is an evil spirit come to destroy our camp!" she whispered loud.

Placing an ear close to the open baby mouth, the chieftain and his wife, each in turn heard the voices of a great camp. The singing of men and women, the beating of the drum, the rattling of deer-hoofs strung like bells on a string, these were the sounds they heard.

"We must go away," said the chieftain, leading them into the night. Out in the open he whispered to the frightened young woman: "Iya, the camp-eater, has come in the guise of a babe.

Had you gone to sleep, he would have jumped out into his own shape and would have devoured our camp. He is a giant with spindling legs. He cannot fight, for he cannot run. He is powerful only in the night with his tricks. We are safe as soon as day breaks." Then moving closer to the woman, he whispered: "If he wakes now, he will swallow the whole tribe with one hideous gulp! Come, we must flee with our people."

Thus creeping from teepee to teepee a secret alarm signal was given. At midnight the teepees were gone and there was left no sign of the village save heaps of dead ashes. So quietly had the people folded their wigwams and bundled their tent poles that they slipped away unheard by the sleeping Iya babe.

When the morning sun arose, the babe awoke. Seeing himself deserted, he threw off his baby form in a hot rage.

Wearing his own ugly shape, his huge body toppled to and fro, from side to side, on a pair of thin legs far too small for their burden. Though with every move he came dangerously nigh to falling, he followed in the trail of the fleeing people.

"I shall eat you in the sight of a noon-day sun!" cried Iya in his vain rage, when he spied them encamped beyond a river.

By some unknown cunning he swam the river and sought his way toward the teepees.

"Hin! hin!" he grunted and growled. With perspiration beading his brow he strove to wiggle his slender legs beneath his giant form.

"Ha! ha!" laughed all the village people to see Iya made foolish with anger. "Such spindle legs cannot stand to fight by daylight!" shouted the brave ones who were terror-struck the night before by the name "Iya."

Warriors with long knives rushed forth and slew the camp-eater.

Lo! there rose out of the giant a whole Indian tribe: their camp ground, their teepees in a large circle, and the people laughing and dancing.

"We are glad to be free!" said these strange people.

Thus Iya was killed; and no more are the camp grounds in danger of being swallowed up in a single night time.

# MANŠTIN, THE RABBIT

MANŠTIN WAS AN adventurous brave, but very kind-hearted. Stamping a moccasined foot as he drew on his buckskin leggins, he said: "Grandmother, beware of Iktomi! Do not let him lure you into some cunning trap. I am going to the North country on a long hunt."

With these words of caution to the bent old rabbit grandmother with whom he had lived since he was a tiny babe, Manštin started off toward the north. He was scarce over the great high hills when he heard the shrieking of a human child.

"Wän!" he ejaculated, pointing his long ears toward the direction of the sound; "Wän! that is the work of cruel Double-Face. Shameless coward! he delights in torturing helpless creatures!"

Muttering indistinct words, Manštin ran up the last hill and lo! in the ravine beyond stood the terrible monster with a face in front and one in the back of his head!

This brown giant was without clothes save for a wild-cat-skin about his loins. With a wicked gleaming eye, he watched the little black-haired baby he held in his strong arm. In a laughing voice he hummed an Indian mother's lullaby, "Ä-bōō! Ä-bōō!" and at the same time he switched the naked baby with a thorny wild-rose bush.

Quickly Manštin jumped behind a large sage bush on the brow of the hill. He bent his bow and the sinewy string twanged. Now an arrow stuck above the ear of Double-Face. It was a poisoned arrow, and the giant fell dead. Then Manštin took the little brown baby and hurried away from the ravine. Soon he came to a teepee from whence loud wailing voices broke. It was the teepee of the stolen baby and the mourners were its heart-broken parents.

When gallant Manštin returned the child to the eager arms of the mother there came a sudden terror into the eyes of both the

Dakotas. They feared lest it was Double-Face come in a new guise to torture them. The rabbit understood their fear and said: "I am Manstin, the kind-hearted,—Manstin, the noted huntsman. I am your friend. Do not fear."

That night a strange thing happened. While the father and mother slept, Manstin took the wee baby. With his feet placed gently yet firmly upon the tiny toes of the little child, he drew upward by each small hand the sleeping child till he was a full-grown man. With a forefinger he traced a slit in the upper lip; and when on the morrow the man and woman awoke they could not distinguish their own son from Manstin, so much alike were the braves.

"Henceforth we are friends, to help each other," said Manstin, shaking a right hand in farewell. "The earth is our common ear, to carry from its uttermost extremes one's slightest wish for the other!"

"Ho! Be it so!" answered the newly made man.

Upon leaving his friend, Manstin hurried away toward the North country whither he was bound for a long hunt. Suddenly he came upon the edge of a wide brook. His alert eye caught sight of a rawhide rope staked to the water's brink, which led away toward a small round hut in the distance. The ground was trodden into a deep groove beneath the loosely drawn rawhide rope.

"Hun-hĕ!" exclaimed Manstin, bending over the freshly made footprints in the moist bank of the brook. "A man's footprints!" he said to himself. "A blind man lives in yonder hut! This rope is his guide by which he comes for his daily water!" surmised Manstin, who knew all the peculiar contrivances of the people. At once his eyes became fixed upon the solitary dwelling and hither he followed his curiosity,—a real blind man's rope.

Quietly he lifted the door-flap and entered in. An old toothless grandfather, blind and shaky with age, sat upon the ground. He was not deaf however. He heard the entrance and felt the presence of some stranger.

"How, grandchild," he mumbled, for he was old enough to be grandparent to every living thing, "how! I cannot see you. Pray, speak your name!"

"Grandfather, I am Manstin," answered the rabbit, all the while looking with curious eyes about the wigwam.

"Grandfather, what is it so tightly packed in all these buckskin bags placed against the tent poles?" he asked.

"My grandchild, those are dried buffalo meat and venison. These are magic bags which never grow empty. I am blind and cannot go on a hunt. Hence a kind Maker has given me these magic bags of choicest foods."

Then the old, bent man pulled at a rope which lay by his right hand. "This leads me to the brook where I drink! and this," said he, turning to the one on his left, "and this takes me into the forest, where I feel about for dry sticks for my fire."

"Grandfather, I wish I lived in such sure luxury! I would lean back against a tent pole, and with crossed feet I would smoke sweet willow bark the rest of my days," sighed Manstin.

"My grandchild, your eyes are your luxury! you would be unhappy without them!" the old man replied.

"Grandfather, I would give you my two eyes for your place!" cried Manstin.

"How! you have said it. Arise. Take out your eyes and give them to me. Henceforth you are at home here in my stead."

At once Manstin took out both his eyes and the old man put them on! Rejoicing, the old grandfather started away with his young eyes while the blind rabbit filled his dream pipe, leaning lazily against the tent pole. For a short time it was a most pleasant pastime to smoke willow bark and to eat from the magic bags.

Manstin grew thirsty, but there was no water in the small dwelling. Taking one of the rawhide ropes he started toward the brook to quench his thirst. He was young and unwilling to trudge slowly in the old man's footpath. He was full of glee, for it had been many long moons since he had tasted such good food. Thus he skipped confidently along, jerking the old weather-eaten rawhide spasmodically till all of a sudden it gave way and Manstin fell headlong into the water.

"Ĕn! Ĕn!" he grunted, kicking frantically amid stream. All along the slippery bank he vainly tried to climb, till at last he chanced upon the old stake and the deeply worn footpath. Exhausted and inwardly disgusted with his mishaps, he crawled more cautiously on all fours to his wigwam door. Dripping with his recent plunge, he sat with chattering teeth within his unfired wigwam.

The sun had set and the night air was chilly, but there was no fire-wood in the dwelling. "Hin!" murmured Manstin and bravely tried the other rope. "I go for some fire-wood!" he said, following the rawhide rope which led into the forest. Soon he stumbled upon thickly strewn dry willow sticks. Eagerly with both hands he gathered the wood into his outspread blanket. Manstin was naturally an energetic fellow.

When he had a large heap, he tied two opposite ends of blanket together and lifted the bundle of wood upon his back, but alas! he had unconsciously dropped the end of the rope and now he was lost in the wood!

"Hin! hin!" he groaned. Then pausing a moment, he set his fan-like ears to catch any sound of approaching footsteps. There was none. Not even a night bird twittered to help him out of his predicament.

With a bold face, he made a start at random.

He fell into some tangled wood where he was held fast. Manstin let go his bundle and began to lament having given away his two eyes.

"Friend, my friend, I have need of you! The old oak tree grandfather has gone off with my eyes and I am lost in the woods!" he cried with his lips close to the earth.

Scarcely had he spoken when the sound of voices was audible on the outer edge of the forest. Nearer and louder grew the voices—one was the clear flute tones of a young brave and the other the tremulous squeaks of an old grandfather.

It was Manstin's friend with the Earth Ear and the old grandfather. "Here Manstin, take back your eyes," said the old man, "I knew you would not be content in my stead, but I wanted you to learn your lesson. I have had pleasure seeing with your eyes and trying your bow and arrows, but since I am old and feeble I much prefer my own teepee and my magic bags!"

Thus talking the three returned to the hut. The old grandfather crept into his wigwam, which is often mistaken for a mere oak tree by little Indian girls and boys.

Manstin, with his own bright eyes fitted into his head again, went on happily to hunt in the North country.

# THE WARLIKE SEVEN

ONCE SEVEN PEOPLE went out to make war,—the Ashes, the Fire, the Bladder, the Grasshopper, the Dragon Fly, the Fish, and the Turtle. As they were talking excitedly, waving their fists in violent gestures, a wind came and blew the Ashes away. "Ho!" cried the others, "he could not fight, this one!"

The six went on running to make war more quickly. They descended a deep valley, the Fire going foremost until they came to a river. The Fire said "Hsss—tchu!" and was gone. "Ho!" hooted the others, "he could not fight, this one!"

Therefore the five went on the more quickly to make war. They came to a great wood. While they were going through it, the Bladder was heard to sneer and to say, "Hĕ! you should rise above these, brothers." With these words he went upward among the tree-tops; and the thorn apple pricked him. He fell through the branches and was nothing! "You see this!" said the four, "this one could not fight."

Still the remaining warriors would not turn back. The four went boldly on to make war. The Grasshopper with his cousin, the Dragon Fly, went foremost. They reached a marshy place, and the mire was very deep. As they waded through the mud, the Grass-hopper's legs stuck, and he pulled them off! He crawled upon a log and wept, "You see me, brothers, I cannot go!"

The Dragon Fly went on, weeping for his cousin. He would not be comforted, for he loved his cousin dearly. The more he grieved, the louder he cried, till his body shook with great violence. He blew his red swollen nose with a loud noise so that his head came off his slender neck, and he was fallen upon the grass.

"You see how it is, said the Fish, lashing his tail impatiently, "these people were not warriors!" "Come!" he said, "let us go on to make war."

Thus the Fish and the Turtle came to a large camp ground.

"Ho!" exclaimed the people of this round village of teepees, "Who are these little ones? What do they seek?"

Neither of the warriors carried weapons with them, and their unimposing stature misled the curious people.

The Fish was spokesman. With a peculiar omission of syllables, he said: "Shu . . . hi pi!"

"Wän! what? what?" clamored eager voices of men and women. Again the Fish said: "Shu . . . hi pi!" Everywhere stood young and old with a palm to an ear. Still no one guessed what the Fish had mumbled!

From the bewildered crowd witty old Iktomi came forward. "Hĕ, listen!" he shouted, rubbing his mischievous palms together, for where there was any trouble brewing, he was always in the midst of it.

"This little strange man says, 'Zuya unhipi! We come to make war!'"

"Ŭun!" resented the people, suddenly stricken glum. "Let us kill the silly pair! They can do nothing! They do not know the meaning of the phrase. Let us build a fire and boil them both!"

"If you put us on to boil," said the Fish, "there will be trouble."

"Ho ho!" laughed the village folk. "We shall see."

And so they made a fire.

"I have never been so angered!" said the Fish. The Turtle in a whispered reply said: "We shall die!"

When a pair of strong hands lifted the Fish over the sputtering water, he put his mouth downward. "Whssh!" he said. He blew the water all over the people, so that many were burned and could not see. Screaming with pain, they ran away.

"Oh, what shall we do with these dreadful ones?" they said.

Others exclaimed: "Let us carry them to the lake of muddy water and drown them!"

Instantly they ran with them. They threw the Fish and the Turtle into the lake. Toward the center of the large lake the Turtle dived. There he peeped up out of the water and, waving a hand at the crowd, sang out, "This is where I live!"

The Fish swam hither and thither with such frolicsome darts that his back fin made the water fly. "Ĕ han!" whooped the Fish, "this is where I live!"

"Oh, what have we done!" said the frightened people, "this will be our undoing."

Then a wise chief said: "Iya, the Eater, shall come and swallow the lake!"

So one went running. He brought Iya, the Eater; and Iya drank all day at the lake till his belly was like the earth. Then the Fish and the Turtle dived into the mud; and Iya said: "They are not in me." Hearing this the people cried greatly.

Iktomi wading in the lake had been swallowed like a gnat in the water. Within the great Iya he was looking skyward. So deep was the water in the Eater's stomach that the surface of the swallowed lake almost touched the sky.

"I will go that way," said Iktomi, looking at the concave within arm's reach.

He struck his knife upward in the Eater's stomach, and the water falling out drowned those people of the village.

Now when the great water fell into its own bed, the Fish and the Turtle came to the shore. They went home painted victors and loud-voiced singers.